ADVANCE PRAISE

"Scott Nadelson's *Trust Me* is, simply, one of the most affecting novels I've read in years. In the midst of busy days, the book waiting for me on my bedside shelf, I found myself missing these characters—how wise and wounded they are, how silly and confused, how fundamentally human. I was hoping for them. *Trust Me* is a book that will have you hoping for us all. Lewis and Skye and the river they share will long stay with me."

—Joe Wilkins, author of *The Entire Sky*

"Scott Nadelson has a remarkable ability to let his characters love and laugh and fumble and grow and burn and bleed right on the page. Alternating between the perspective of a recently divorced father and his teenage daughter, we follow two intertwined lives as they each awkwardly find their way. It's a gift to witness the humanity of this story. *Trust me.*"

—Yuvi Zalkow, author of *I Only Cry in Emoticons*

"*Trust Me* is an exquisite novel: tender, funny, and wonderfully absorbing. Nadelson shows us a father and daughter marked by the seasons, pressed to redefine themselves in the world and with each other in luminous, spirited prose."

—Elizabeth McKenzie, author of *The Dog of the North*

"Scott Nadelson beautifully, movingly sketches the balance between turbulence and poise, wonder and boredom, bravery and vulnerability that is being twelve, or raising someone who is twelve, and perfectly captures the muddled marvel of feeling like a child, while also feeling like an adult, which is true here of both father and daughter and, as we read, maybe all of us."

—Laurie Frankel, author of *One Two Three*

"Scott Nadelson's *Trust Me* is tender and impossibly wise, a soulful tapestry of fifty-two moving vignettes depicting the unbreakable yet eternally fraught bonds between fathers and teenage daughters. Watching Lewis and Skye circle one another amid the buffeting waves of adolescence, divorce, isolation, wildfires, and more, Nadelson reminds us (to every parent's chagrin) that the only constant is change. He is a compassionate, witty, and attentive observer of these fundamental familial ties."

—Mark Sarvas, author of *Memento Park*

PRAISE FOR PAST WORK

"Nadelson is a short form master and magician."

—Cris Mazza, author of *Charlatan: New and Selected Stories*

"These are ripping good tales by a remarkably gifted writer."

— Josh Weil, author of *The Age of Perpetual Light*

"With grace, ease, and astounding sensitivity, Nadelson squires us through a dazzling array of human experience and emotion reminding us again the power and majesty of great stories."

—Gina Ochsner, author of *The Hidden Letters of Velta B.*

"Nadelson reports on the human condition with joy, humor, and lapidary insightfulness."

—Christine Sneed, author of *Paris, He Said*

"Scott Nadelson has an uncanny way of getting under the skin of his characters and capturing the day-to-day rhythms of complex lives. His people may think of themselves as ordinary, but they are anything but. They're survivors—and the stakes here are high.

—Peter Orner, author of *Last Car Over the Sagamore Bridge*

TRUST ME

A NOVEL

SCOTT NADELSON

FOREST AVENUE PRESS
Portland, Oregon

Library of Congress Cataloging-in-Publication Data

Names: Nadelson, Scott, author.
Title: Trust me / Scott Nadelson.
Description: Portland, Oregon : Forest Avenue Press, 2024. | Summary: "As a last-ditch effort to save his marriage, Lewis--an East Coast suburban Jew who has run from his roots--buys a cabin on a wild and scenic river in the Cascade foothills; after the marriage falls apart, he moves to the woods and makes the long commute every morning to Salem, the state capital, where he works a tedious government job. Skye stays with him on weekends, leaving behind her middle-school friends, her cellular service, her cat, and her mom in exchange for ancient trees and clear water and moss-covered rocks. In fifty-two vignettes-one for each week of the year-that alternate between Lewis's perspective and Skye's, the novel traces their days foraging for mushrooms and searching for newts, arguing over jigsaw puzzles and confronting menacing neighbors, hosting skeptical visitors and taking city jaunts, finding pleasure in small moments of wonder and coping with devastating loss. By turns comic and heartbreaking, Trust Me is a study of the uneasy bond between a hapless father and his precocious daughter, of their love for a complex and changing landscape, of the necessity and precariousness of the relationships and places we cherish most"-- Provided by publisher.
Identifiers: LCCN 2024008243 (print) | LCCN 2024008244 (ebook) | ISBN 9781942436638 (trade paperback) | ISBN 9781942436645 (ebook)
Subjects: LCSH: Fathers and daughters--Fiction. | LCGFT: Novels.
Classification: LCC PS3614.A34 T78 2024 (print) | LCC PS3614.A34 (ebook) | DDC 813/.6--dc23/eng/20240223
LC record available at https://lccn.loc.gov/2024008243
LC ebook record available at https://lccn.loc.gov/2024008244

Distributed by Publishers Group West
Printed in the U.S.

Forest Avenue Press LLC
P.O. Box 80134
Portland, OR 97280
forestavenuepress.com

1 2 3 4 5 6 7 8 9

For Iona and the Little North Fork.

TRUST ME

FALL

1. KEYS

It's a Monday morning, end of September, the south-facing windows catching only the first dim flush of sunrise. Outside, the ground wet from yesterday's rain steams between ferns washed free of dust. Beyond them the river, still low between its banks, carries sticks and the first downed leaves of fall.

Lewis needs more light, but he doesn't want to turn on a lamp. Instead he waits for his eyes to adjust, and when they don't, he searches with his hands, pawing the dining table, the cold stone of the mantel, the top of the shoe rack. He has the couch cushions flipped up, fingers running over crumbs beneath, when his daughter comes out of her bedroom.

"Lost them again," she says. A statement, not a question. She's dressed for school in a sweatshirt that's too baggy, jeans too tight, hair damp. Her name is Skye, but since she was an infant, he's called her Silly, or Sills for short.

"I didn't lose them. I just don't remember where they are."

"Last time they were in your jacket."

"I checked already." When she turns to scan the bookshelf,

he hurries to the coatrack. Did he wear the leather jacket last night? Or the fleece? He jams his hands into the pockets of both but comes up with nothing. She's watching him when he glances up. "I knew they weren't there," he says.

"Why don't you at least put the lights on?"

"I probably left them in the car," Lewis says. "Grab some breakfast. We're leaving as soon as I find them."

"Check on the path," Sills says. "You might've dropped them on your way in. Again."

She has one hand on her hip, head tilted to the left so her hair falls across her neck. The way her braces push out her lips gives her mouth a permanent pout, made sour by the scrunching of her eyes. It's a disconcerting look not only because it resembles the one Veronica turned on him so often in the last years of their marriage—when she was debating how long she could stay in it—but because it sits on Sills's face so naturally. Only twelve, and she doesn't have to work to make him squirm. Twelve and a half, that is. She reminds him every time he objects to her sitting in the car alone while he goes into a store, or to her walking by herself to the diner on the highway where, if he doesn't order a burger and salad for her, she'll eat nothing but a shake and fries. *I'm twelve and a half for crying out loud*, she'll say, and he'll reply, *Exactly*, before walking with her to the diner, though its food gives him cramps.

He takes the path slowly, shuffling his feet, hoping to hear the click of keys without having to bend down to search. But the only sound is the crackle and whisper of skeletal weeds. He nudges some of the nearby ferns with his foot, but still nothing. The light has come up enough to splinter on the crack in his driver's side window, but the river is still in shadow. To his relief, the car door is unlocked, but the keys aren't in the ignition as he hoped. Not on the floor, either, or between the seats.

He pictures that disgruntled look on Sills's face, Veronica's look, and wonders again how long it will be before she tells him she can't come with him this weekend; she doesn't want to miss her soccer game or ballet recital or a trip to the mall with her friends. He feels the familiar pinch of looming loss along with a terrible urge to kick something and run. Why do even the smallest things have to be so difficult?

"Hey! Mr. Observant!"

She stands in the doorway, backlit by the kitchen window, her silhouette less like her mother's now than that of a stranger who appeared without invitation in the cabin he bought so optimistically a year ago, when he still believed he could control the future by wishing it a certain way.

"Use your eyes much?" Sills calls, her face still in shadow.

Then, with a sudden movement that makes him start, she swings the door closed. Lewis is left standing among the ferns, their fronds lush for the first time since early summer, the spiderwebs strung between them jeweled with raindrops. Is she locking him out? Then he hears before he sees: a jingle coming from the door. The keys, still swaying beneath the knob.

He retrieves them and then his jacket—the leather one, though he can tell already it will be too warm by midday. He glances around for windows he needs to lock, for burners he needs to shut off for the eleven hours he'll be gone. On the coffee table is a nail polish stain—hot pink, a color Veronica hates—next to a plate of mostly uneaten cake.

Last night he tried to make a celebration. A year since they bought the cabin. *Our cabin*, he said, bringing out the cake he'd picked up at Safeway a week earlier and hid at the back of the freezer. *Happy anniversary*, Sills replied, took two bites of frosting, and then went to work on her nails. The word *anniversary* struck him as wrong, but he didn't come up with a different one. Had it really been a year since they first walked these floors and lit the woodstove?

If I can just make it through the first year, I'll survive, he's been telling himself since he moved out of the house, whenever he thinks he can't make it through another day. What's he supposed to tell himself when the year is past?

"You should always leave them there," Sills says, backpack over one shoulder, hands searching or arranging the contents of a black purse with silver embellishments, a pear tucked under her chin. "Never forget where they are that way."

"Is that all you're eating?"

"Not like anyone's gonna break in here."

"You'll be hungry in an hour."

"I mean, can you imagine? Dumbest burglar on the planet. Come out to the middle of nowhere looking for places to rob? What are they gonna steal, your fishing rod?"

She finds what she's looking for in the purse—a lipstick tube, which she runs over her mouth three times. The same hideous shade as her nails. Something else for Veronica to hold against him.

"I put a granola bar in your lunch. You can eat it on the way."

"That should be their reward. Drive all the way out here to rip us off, might as well have the keys in the door. Come on in."

"This isn't the middle of nowhere," he says. "We're twenty minutes from Millburg."

"Booming metropolis."

"Forty-five from the state capital."

"Likewise."

"And fly rods aren't cheap. A new one costs a thousand bucks."

"No wonder."

"What's that supposed to mean?"

"You didn't pay for ballet last month."

"I just forgot. How many times do I have to apologize?"
Sills mumbles something he doesn't catch.

"Forty-five minutes," he says and glances at his wrist. No
watch. Who knows where it is? He has no time to look for it
now. "We've got to go this instant."

She pushes past him, slinging her purse over her free shoulder and taking a bite from the pear. But once outside, she doesn't
head for the car. Instead she cuts off the path, passes the stack of
wood that needs splitting, winds between the ferns and under
the firs. For a moment he loses her in the shadows.

"Hey! I said right now!"

She ignores him. Her footsteps crunch through the underbrush, and then she appears again in a patch of sunlight just
above the riverbank. But before he can shout again, she's
climbed down to the gravel beach that stretches a dozen yards
into the bend. He follows, cursing, the legs of his chinos quickly
growing damp from the brush of wet ferns. The cuffs are sop-
ping by the time he reaches her.

"What the hell don't you understand about now?" His
voice sounds strained and thin, as if coming through a long
pipe plugged at one end with mud.

She picks up a stone and tosses it into the water, which ripples here and there over midsize rocks. Past the bend it's still
deep enough to form a pool even before the rains come in ear-
nest next month. They swam in it all summer, and now he longs
for those hot, languid days, even tinged as they were with grief.
Will it really be most of a year before the heat returns? All those
days and weeks and months?

She still says nothing, keeping her face angled away from him. She doesn't want him to see what's on it. This is far worse than her open stare. Veronica turned away from him, too, just before the end, to hide what she wasn't yet ready to say. The panic bubbles up once more. Isn't what he already lost enough? In his mind, he's compromising with her: *if it's better for you, we can make it every other weekend . . .*

"I won't see it again for five days," Sills says, waving a hand at the river and sniffing hard.

"You can't be late again," he says.

"I always miss it when we leave."

Even as he's taking in what she said, he's speaking, out of instinct, and telling himself to shut up. "I can't have the school calling your mother—"

"It doesn't matter," she says. "She's gonna be mad at you either way."

"You always miss it?"

"So you might as well stop trying so hard."

"Did she tell you that?"

"It's obvious."

He almost laughs. "Jesus, Sills. Do you have to know so much? Can't you act your age?" He reaches out to ruffle her hair, but she bats his hand away.

"Quit messing with me, will you?"

He fingers the keys in his pocket, but the urgency to leave dwindles as the water brightens. She'll miss the river for the five days she won't see it. What else can he ask for? He knows better than to hope for more than he deserves. She tosses another stone, trying to reach the pool but falling short.

"I guess we better go," she says.

"Whenever you're ready."

They watch the leaves and twigs bob past, a few twirling in the eddies. Soon the light spills over the trees on the far bank and strikes the water, flashing on ripples and turning the still parts clear all the way to the bottom.

2. PUZZLE

WHEN SHE'S AT HOME in Salem, Skye is mostly sure she loves her mother more than her father. Even when they're fighting, usually over clothes Skye covets that her mother doesn't want to buy, she doesn't question her feelings. Without thinking about it very consciously, she's come to consider her mother an extension of herself, or maybe she an extension of her mother. Both are long-limbed and sandy-haired with an appreciation for order and an attention to visual details, each obsessively rearranging objects in her respective sphere: her mother the flowers in a vase on the dining room table, Skye the collection of feathers—from a blue jay and a goldfinch, both murdered by a neighbor's cat; her own cat, Verlaine, is too old to catch anything that flies higher than the seat of his favorite chair— pinned to her bedroom wall.

She never has to ask herself whether or not she loves her mother. The love is just there, an undercurrent to her drab days at school, her evenings of plodding through seventh-grade homework or watching TV or texting with friends during the one hour her mother allows her to use her phone.

It isn't that she believes she needs to love one parent more than another, just that she does, naturally, because one is easier to love. Her mother is comfortably predictable, serious but affectionate, a setter of rules Skye can follow or flail against when necessary. When Skye relates some drama among her friends—"Aliyah won't sit next to Kendall because Kendall called her an attention whore"—she asks irritating mom-questions, like, "Can't you figure out a way to bring them together?" which of course is beside the point. What Skye wants to talk about is whether Aliyah really is an attention whore, or if Kendall was the one whoring for attention by saying so to the whole lunch table. So instead of answering the question, she says, "It must be so boring to be old," which makes her mother scowl pleasurably.

But staying at the cabin confuses her, complicates her sense of order. For one, she still thinks of the place as their family getaway rather than her father's house. When they drive the forty-five minutes out of town, snaking up the river until the woods close around them for the weekend, she still in her ballet tights and leotard, it seems to her that he's driving in the wrong direction, that he's forgotten the way and is getting them lost. And then she asks, silently, *Do I love him?* before answering, *Right now I do*. That loving him isn't something she takes for granted unnerves her, but the tenuousness also makes the love more present. She can't just ignore it, as she does with her mother, because one day it might disappear.

So she finds herself watching him as he goes about his morning routine, muttering to himself, bumping into furniture until he's had his first sips of coffee, then preparing something out of his range for breakfast—pancakes with fresh huckleberries they picked on a recent hike—only to realize after he's mixed most of it in a bowl that he doesn't have some essential ingredient—baking powder, milk—and finally cooking it anyway and pretending to enjoy it while Skye takes a single bite before switching to yogurt and store-bought fruit. In the wake of his effort, a colossal mess will linger all weekend if she doesn't clean it up.

Who is this person she spends sixty-three hours with every week? He looks nothing like her, with his dark, curly hair and wide mouth and dimpled chin, his cheeks growing more shadowed as the weekend goes on, until finally he scrapes away the bristles before returning her to the world—usually late—on Monday morning. All they share are long fingers and toes, bony wrists and ankles, crowded teeth which her braces are now straightening. His, straightened decades ago, have since drifted into an overbite.

Almost everything he does seems strange to her. He spends hours picking out bird feeders and arranging them on the back deck but then never remembers to check them. If she doesn't fill them with seed every couple of weeks, they'll stay empty all summer. But when the birds come swooping out of the woods, he'll watch them for an entire afternoon, mesmerized, their wings and stabbing beaks holding his interest in a way little else does.

He's that way with other things too. One Sunday every month he toils over bills and his checkbook and then leaves the sealed envelopes, unstamped, on the shoe rack for weeks. He tells Skye she's the most important thing in his life but missed her most recent recital, in which she played one of Peter Pan's lost children, because he wrote down the wrong date on his calendar.

Still, they have some things in common, things they like to

do together. Swimming in the river on hot days. Building cairns on the bank. Laboring over jigsaw puzzles, the more challenging the better. They usually save them for evenings, but today, because it's raining and because her father's back hurts too much for him to stand in the river fishing, they pull out a puzzle after breakfast, a big one he picked out on his last shopping trip in town. A thousand pieces that together will form the image of a peacock, its head and neck in the foreground with a spread of feathers behind.

At the start it's slow going. The feathers are hard to distinguish from each other, and the neck is a solid stretch of blue with only a subtle shift in shade from top to bottom. But they work well together, each with a different strategy: her father focuses on the edges while Skye sorts pieces by color before moving methodically from section to section. So far, they have half the frame complete, plus the peacock's head, and it isn't yet noon. At this pace, if it keeps raining, they'll finish by dinner. There's evidence of their past success around them. Her father figured out a way to glue the backs of puzzles onto newspaper and hang them, and here above the table is a jumble of brightly colored popsicles, and over the couch a display of toy trains. More puzzles are in her bedroom: one of Cracker Jacks, another of tulips, a third of sleeping kittens.

She knows, too, that he spends a long time shopping for them, choosing only images she's sure to like, bypassing cut-up Cézanne paintings and photos of rivers and mountains. Why would you want something on the wall you can see out the window? Despite all her mother's complaints about his self-ishness and inconsistency, he's considerate in this regard. But now his forehead is creased, and his whole body bends forward as he scours the scattered pieces for flat sides, not paying attention when his head blocks the light and makes it hard for her to see.

"Sure you don't have any edges in there?" he asks, running his fingers through one of her piles.

"Posture, Dad."

"I'm still missing two corners."

"You'll complain about your back all day tomorrow."

"I never complain. I just report."

He keeps fishing around on her side until she pushes his arm away and tells him to keep out of her bubble space, a concept she learned in kindergarten and has often used against him. *Everyone's bubble space is different,* she once told him at six or seven years old, deciding on that day, angry at him for reasons she can no longer remember, that hers took up the whole house. *Daddy,* she'd said, *I'm afraid you'll have to go outside.*

Now, when he backs out of her light, she tries out the gossip that fell flat with her mother. What did he think, was Aliyah the attention whore, or Kendall?

"It depends," he answers. "When Kendall said it, did she toss her head like this, and make sure everyone was looking at her?"

"More like this," Skye says and flings her ponytail over a shoulder.

"Total attention whore."

"That's what I thought."

"I wouldn't sit next to her either," her father says.

"Here's your corner."

She tosses it to him, a little blue wedge with which he connects the puzzle's left side to the bottom. Then he's digging in her piles again and blocking the light, his head casting a shadow over the peacock's neck. "The other one's got to be in here too," he says, and as Skye leans away to give him room, she finds herself beginning to cry. Yes, right now, she loves him. But the problem is he expects her to, even if she doesn't. The fragments of peacock blur together into a puddle of shifting color.

She jabs him with an elbow. "Out of my bubble," she says.

3. REAL ESTATE

HE CAME ACROSS THE listing soon after their first brief separation, when Veronica agreed to give their marriage another chance. A perfect little A-frame with a bedroom for Sills downstairs, a loft for him and Veronica above, and a view of the river through a screen of Douglas fir and big-leaf maple. For a few weeks he kept it to himself, watching the price fall, clicking through the pictures online, fantasizing about the life they'd live when they owned it. A Hail Mary, his therapist called it, which irritated him enough that he canceled his next two appointments.

"We can't take anything for granted," he said to Veronica a day or two after he finally sent her the link. "This is the only life we've got."

By then she was wavering, intrigued yet still fretting over their finances and whether they could really afford a second mortgage, even a small one, and what about upkeep? His words had their intended effect, bringing a flush to her cheeks that reminded him of their early days together, when they'd followed every whim—most of them his—and couldn't be in a room together without touching. Or later, when they named their first and only child after an island they hoped one day to visit. With a familiar and comforting abandon, he picked up the phone, called the realtor, and made an offer.

But they'd spent only three weekends here over four months, agreeing that it was the perfect place except for the plumbing clearly installed by someone without a license—there was a drip under the kitchen sink, and the toilet needed plunging nearly every time he took a dump—before Veronica decided their bond was frayed beyond repair. By then he was out of ideas to change her mind. All her claims against him were true. Yes, he was impulsive and forgetful. Yes, he was terrible with money. No, he didn't like to think about the future. "Don't we still have fun together?" he asked. She didn't answer.

Rather than take an apartment in town and unload the cabin, which the realtor assured him he could do at only a 20 percent loss—that is, if he first replaced the shoddy plumbing— he moved all his things out to the woods and now makes the long commute every weekday morning. On Fridays he picks Sills up after dance practice and sits in traffic, listening to her grumble about being hungry and bored. After they clear the cars clogging the I-5 on-ramp and move swiftly out of town, he listens to her fiddle with the radio and complain when every station fuzzes with static. He has no TV in the cabin, no internet, and unreliable cell service. *It's good for her to get out of the city, breathe some clean air, cut off the media,* he tells Veronica. But he knows she considers living in the cabin one more example of his childishness, his refusal to grow up and participate in a world that doesn't value his instinct for the impractical. His therapist agrees. Getting rid of the place would be a positive step in his healing process, she told him soon after the divorce was finalized, and he should focus instead on his daughter's needs. After that he stopped going to appointments altogether.

When they finally arrive, the sun sinking behind trees to the west, Sills paces the deck, holding her cell phone at arm's length, trying to find a signal. "Come on," she says, shaking the phone and moving it a few inches to the left. "Come on, you stupid thing." If she gets a bar or two, she'll spend the next hour typing furiously with her thumbs, telling some friend how bored she was on the drive out, how she can't believe she has to spend all weekend in the woods, how she has no one to talk to and nothing to do. She leans over the deck railing, but still no luck. Lewis says a little prayer of thanks to the distant cell phone tower, brings her bag inside, sets a pot of water on the stove. When he remembers, he checks the landline phone for messages. He's given the number to only a handful of people, and usually the voice mail is empty, except maybe for a message from his parents, or one from Veronica reminding him to pay a bill, or a political robocall telling him to vote for a state senate candidate he's never heard of.

Tonight, though, to his surprise, he hears a woman's voice, one he doesn't at first recognize. It speaks quickly, leaving a number and asking him to call back as soon as possible. Though urgent, it's also a pleasantly husky voice, and for the first time in months he feels not only hopeful but mildly aroused, and he fails to listen to most of the words. The voice sparks images of a fire in the woodstove, a blanket on the floor, legs tangled underneath.

But when he plays the message a second time, he understands who it is and what she wants: his realtor, telling him the market is coming back, Portlanders searching for a summer getaway, Californians looking to escape the drought, investors snatching up rental properties. She thinks she can get multiple offers, start a bidding war to bump above the asking price, and then once they accept, they can negotiate to cover the plumbing. He stands to make a tidy profit, she says. The cabin has turned out to be quite a nice investment, even, she adds a little sheepishly, if she argued against it at the time. Maybe she'd start coming to him for advice.

He'd play it a third time if Veronica were here to listen. *See?* he'd say and accept her grudging acknowledgment that not every decision he made was a bad one. Even better, he thinks, he'll sell the place and, without telling Veronica, put all the profit into Sills's college fund; she'll check the account and see its value suddenly doubled. But other fantasies compete with this one: pocketing the cash, quitting his job writing press releases and internal newsletters for the Department of Transportation, disappearing for a year or two on a trek around the world. Of course he'll take Sills with him for part of it, when she isn't in school. On his own, he'll meet local women who might offer him a place to sleep for a night or two. He finds the realtor's card in a kitchen drawer, stares at her phone number, then glances around at the cabin's sparse furniture, at the small appliances he can sell or give away, at the many books he can put in storage. What does he have, aside from his child, that he can't leave behind?

The water on the stove releases a few tentative bubbles from the bottom of the pot, but they haven't yet reached the surface. Through the window, he can see Sills on the deck, no longer looking at her phone. She's crouched low, creeping forward on bare feet. It takes him a moment to realize she's heading for the hummingbird feeder, where a pair of Anna's slurp sugar water from red plastic flowers, their iridescent green backs catching the last light of day, pink throats flashing when they turn their heads. While he watches, a third comes zipping down from a nearby tree and chases one off, and that one in turn flies straight up until nearly out of sight and then dive-bombs the third. This dance continues as Sills inches closer, until her hair, still in a ballerina's bun, slips within a few inches of the feeder's base.

The birds take no notice of her, or else they don't mind her attention, all three now settling in to sip, their bills deep inside the feeder, heads frozen in place as their wings go translucent. When she's right below them, she reaches up a hand, slowly, slowly, one finger extended until its tip just touches the bottom of the glass cylinder. Then she puts her other hand flat against her throat and crouches that way for three, four seconds, when all at once, as if they've coordinated, the three birds speed off in different directions. Sills keeps both hands where they are. Maybe the vibration continues after they've left. Or maybe she's begun humming to keep the feeling alive.

Now the water has gone to a full rolling boil. Lewis tosses a handful of spaghetti into the pot. Then he picks up the phone, plays the realtor's message again, and deletes it before it's halfway finished.

4. THE KING

THE FIRST MONTH OF fall is her favorite of the year. Since mid-July everything has been sun-scorched and sapped of water, the moss growing brittle, fern leaves curling in the heat, gravel dust kicking up from the road and coating the vine maples along the driveway. But after a few days of rain everything brightens again, as if electrified, while the ground goes dark and pungent with the smell of rotting leaves and fir needles, and mushrooms pop out of the ground everywhere. Some are smaller than the nail of her pinky, others the size of a dinner plate. She loves watching them split the soil and unfurl like little umbrellas over the course of a day or two, and then she spends hours taking pictures of them with her phone, trying to capture them from all angles, not so she can identify them—she's tried using her father's mushroom guide and quickly tires of reading about gill shapes and spore size—only to show off their strangeness and beauty.

But show off to whom? Her friends at school couldn't care less about mushrooms, and if she texted them the pictures, they'd call her *cave girl* or *mountain mama* and think she's even weirder than they already believe. So she keeps them in a separate folder from her other pictures, the selfies before her ballet recitals and the ones in which her friends make funny faces as they wait to board buses after school. She's let her mother scroll through the mushroom snaps a couple of times, and while the latter has made appreciative noises and has complimented Skye's attention to detail—"Ooh, that one's gorgeous," or "You really got the color on this one"—after looking at a dozen or so, her attention wanes, and Skye snatches back her phone.

Her father, on the other hand, will study each one intently, his massive guidebook next to him on one side, on the other a legal pad on which he makes meticulous notes about cap and gills and stem. He's turned it into a project: they'll identify as many as they can, record the variety and richness of their home. And she goes along with it because it means he encourages her to take the pictures, though knowing the Latin names for what she finds is beside the point as far as she's concerned. She prefers the common names, which she repeats to herself during the week, bored in social science class: *fairy saddle, pig's ear, destroying angel*. Mostly she's just amazed by their otherworldliness, these alien life forms that spread secretly underground during spring, wait quietly all summer, and then colonize the land when rain drives people inside. No one else seems to realize how bizarre it is. So she waits until she's in bed at night to scroll through the pictures on her own.

This early in the season, the rain falls intermittently, and there are still enough sun breaks to spend hours by the river or on trails heading up into the surrounding hills. Her father wants a good workout when they hike, and she knows he's frustrated by her pace as she stops every few feet to snap photos. But he also wants them to stay together when they're in the woods—he's reminded her multiple times that people have spotted black bear out here, and cougar, though he's never seen either—so he slows and says nothing. The trees grow thicker as they ascend, some of the Doug fir trunks six feet across, the grooves in their bark deep enough to stick a whole fist in. Others, fallen during storms, have been slowly decomposing for years, blanketed in moss and lichen, fringed with licorice fern, little forests of wild blueberry growing on top, and this is where she often finds the most interesting things to photograph: spiky coral fungus; bright yellow slime molds; a purple mushroom her father describes as lewd, though he won't explain why; another that looks like discarded orange peels.

Occasionally they spot something he wants to take home. Compared to other endeavors—especially those to do with spending money, according to her mother—he's cautious when it comes to eating wild mushrooms. At least he is now. Last year he cooked up a pile of what turned out to be false chanterelles and made himself sick for three days. This year he swears he'll pick only things he's absolutely sure about. Oyster mushrooms growing on alder logs. Chicken of the woods on fir stumps. Lion's mane on a scarred oak. Cauliflower mushrooms that look less like cauliflower than a pile of curly noodles someone swallowed without chewing and then hurled beneath a hemlock. She won't eat any of them, though she enjoys the portabellas he buys from the supermarket and sears on the propane grill.

Today, though, she finds something that excites him more than usual. "Is that what I think it is?" he asks, and then crouches with obvious pain, pressing a hand to his lower back, to scrutinize it from below. It's a big mushroom with a wide brown cap, a stout stem, and a spongy underside rather than gills. "It is," he says. "No question." He claps and whistles. "The king. We're in for a treat tonight."

"Are you sure it's safe?" she asks. "I hate listening to you barf."

"We'll double-check the book. Do a spore print if we have to. But I'm pretty sure."

"Sounds like a wolf coughing up live chickens."

"King bolete. Prize of the woods."

"Last time I thought you were dying. I almost called an ambulance."

"Porcini, baby. You pay big bucks for them in Italian restaurants. And those have usually been sitting around in oil for years."

"Does it have look-alikes? Death king? King of the underworld?"

"We'll look it up and make sure when we get home," he says, his fingers already gripping the stem. "But I'm like 99 percent sure it's the real deal. Maybe 97. But we'll do our due diligence."

"Get your grubby hands off," she says. "I'm not finished yet."

He backs away, and she takes several more shots from different angles. It truly is grand looking, noble even, though when she teases it up from the soil, small black bugs scurry beneath the cap. She's able to brush some off, but at least a few duck into the pores that line the underside.

"We'll soak them out when we get home," her father says before easing it into a sealable plastic bag and tucking it into his backpack. "I'm telling you, Sills, this is one you'll want to try. Best mushroom in the world. Except maybe for the morel. But those don't come until spring. We'll make fresh pasta. Or maybe homemade pizza. If we've got any flour. And cheese. We can probably get most of what we need at the market in Millburg. Hell, we can drive all the way to the Safeway in Stayton if we have to. No point ruining the king with crappy ingredients."

He chatters the whole way down the trail. She hasn't seen him this happy in months, and for that alone she's grateful enough to determine she'll try the mushroom even if it makes her nervous. The black beetles aren't what bother her most—they're hardly bigger than a pinhead—nor even the possibility of eating something poisonous. Rather, it's that she feels she shouldn't take things from the forest, at least not without leaving something in return. But that isn't quite right, either: all summer she picks thimbleberries and huckleberries and sour grass without the slightest compunction. A mushroom, though, is different somehow, belonging to the secret time when the woods are mostly free of people. She wants to make an offering of some kind, but she can't imagine what. Instead she decides she'll get one of these photos printed and hang it on her wall.

When they get back to the cabin, she says she'll clean up the kitchen while he goes to the store. She doesn't want to be in the car, she tells him, or around people, both sentiments he understands and admires. The truth is, she wants more time to arrange and photograph the king. She sets him up on the deck, propped so he appears to be blooming out of the railing, out of a bird feeder, out of the palm of her hand. She arranges him with a little ceramic gnome her father bought years ago as a joke—he'd get up early in the morning and move him around their yard in Salem, and Skye, even though she knew who was behind it, would play along, making a big show of searching and exclaiming over the little guy's magical abilities—and snaps a dozen more photos. She shoots the king on the kitchen table, on the couch, in her bed with her stuffed animals: a goat, a sheep, a sloth. She's quickly come to think of him as a new friend, an adopted family member, and starts to doubt the idea of having him for dinner, though she's caught whiffs of his nutty aroma and finds herself growing hungry.

She doesn't want to disappoint her father, but now she thinks eating the king would be like eating a chicken she raised. She brings him outside again, sets him on a bed of moss beside the path to the river, and takes one last picture. She'll leave him there just until her father gets home, she thinks, a few more minutes in his natural habitat, and now she does tidy the kitchen counter, which is covered in plates from breakfast. If she left it to her father, he'd just pile them all in one corner while he cooked dinner, and they'd be teetering by evening; more than once he's accidentally tipped a stack into the sink and broken whatever was perched on top.

But she isn't at it long before she sees the king again. Through the window over the sink, he should be slightly out of view, except here he is, directly in front of her, in the grip of a squirrel. One of the little brown ones with an orange belly—a native species, her father has told her, unlike the big, gray invasive ones that have taken over the parks in Salem. She knows they're rare, and normally she's happy to see them, but this one is chewing on the king's cap. "Fucking squirrel!" she cries and drops the coffee cup she's been washing. It rolls into the sink but doesn't break, or at least from the sound it makes she doesn't think it's broken but doesn't check to see, because now she's running outside, shouting and waving her arms. The squirrel takes off with the king still clamped between its tiny hands. It ducks beneath a sword fern and then through the prickly leaves of Oregon grape and up the nearest fir, where it perches on the lowest branch, twenty feet above her head. There it squats and munches, giving her its full profile so it can keep her in view. Its teeth work methodically around the edge of the cap, and when that's gone, down the length of the bulbous stalk. Bits of the king rain down and dot the bare soil around the tree's trunk.

She's weeping when her father returns with two bags of groceries, blubbering so incomprehensibly it takes several tries to explain what's happened, punctuating every other statement with "I'll kill that fucking squirrel!" She apologizes several times, says she shouldn't have left it alone, but when he finally understands, he shrugs it off, tells her it isn't her fault, she shouldn't be so hard on herself. Still, she sees the disappointment in his face, stubbled and tired now, a hint of the sorrow he always tries and fails to hide from her darkening his features as he gazes up into the tree.

"Hey," he says, setting down the grocery bags. "It's no big deal." He tries to hug her, but she turns away. "It's just a mushroom. We'll find more, right? At least now we know it really was what I thought it was. Squirrel's got good taste."

Nothing he says consoles her. She left her precious king exposed, let the enemy steal in undetected, and now he's gone inside its horrible orange belly.

"I've got to get these inside," her father says. "I bought ice cream. And I picked up portobellos in case you weren't ready to try the bolete. So we're good. We've got plenty to eat. We'll still make a feast. And you've still got your pictures."

She lets him go inside. She's done crying now, but the anger lingers along with the pain. There's a smell in the air, moist and dank, that wasn't here before, and she guesses it's the scent of the ravaged king. She shouts up the tree, tells the fucking creature what she'll do if she ever catches it. She doesn't care if it's endangered—she'll show it what endangered really means. But the squirrel is gone, either too high up in the branches for her to see, or on another tree, though she didn't witness its escape. She pulls out her phone once more and takes a photo of the carnage on the ground, the scattered white strands, one fingernail-sized chunk of the king's cap against last year's downed needles. This picture she'll show no one.

"Hey," her father calls from the deck, "it's just a fungus, right?"

5. METAPHOR

HIS CLOSEST PERMANENT NEIGHBOR—there are two vacation
rentals between them—owns every power tool ever invented.
As soon as fall arrives, he's out daily with a leaf blower, making
a racket that echoes up and down the canyon and, Lewis
guesses, keeping deer and elk from descending the slopes
until later in the season. If he were a hunter, it might infuriate
him, but he hasn't shot a gun in his life—has never even held
one, unless you count the pellet rifle with which he shattered
a friend's garage window when he was eleven. He's content
with a fly rod instead, which satisfies his masculine desire to
hold on to something solid and precious and requiring skill to
use. The rhythm of casting and watching his leader drift on the
current suits his need for focus, keeps his mind from otherwise
spinning toward despair, and even though he's caught no more
than a dozen rainbows this season, along with a single brown,
it earns him his place on the river, his reason for being here. He
can't claim to belong yet—a New Jersey transplant who spent
his first decade in Oregon living in its largest city, the next in its

state capital—but while standing in the shallows, secure in his waders, he's at home among the trees, at peace whether or not the fish are striking.

Or he would be at peace if not for the sound of the leaf blower, which vibrates up his spine and rattles his skull. It might not scare the fish away, but it makes him want to find a river with no houses for a thousand miles in all directions. It's late October now, and he has only a week and a half before the season ends. He's been planning to spend most of it fishing—he's even taken two vacation days in the coming week—heading for the river as soon as he gets home from work, but every time he does, there's the neighbor—who goes by Gerry, though the name on his business card reads Gerald—making sure not a single leaf or dry needle lies dormant on his driveway or the multiple paths to and from his house. Why move to the woods if you don't want the woods around you?

Now Gerry is at it on a Saturday morning just past ten. Sills is inside doing homework so they can spend the afternoon hiking to a lake where the huckleberry leaves go scarlet this time of year. He's planning to bring his rod there, too, and cast a bit while Sills searches for frogs. But now she appears on the bank above him and shouts, "How'm I supposed to do anything with all that effing noise?" She's got his headphones around her neck, a heavy-duty pair whose pads cover the whole ear, but still her face is pinched with exasperation.

"I'll go talk to him," he says. "Tell him you've got a migraine."

"You don't need to lie."

"It's not a lie. It's metaphorical. The noise makes you feel like you've got a migraine."

"Just tell him if he doesn't turn it off, I'll throw myself in the river. That's literal."

By the time Lewis makes it past the two rentals, several hundred yards downstream, Gerry has swapped leaf blower for chainsaw, which he is using to shear a fallen maple limb into flat rounds that can fit into a stove without splitting. He, too, has headphones on and doesn't hear Lewis approach, so Lewis stands out of the way, seething with hatred.

Gerry does hunt, at least in theory. The one previous time Lewis visited, Gerry showed him his collection of rifles, half a dozen of them, including a semiautomatic that could level a herd. But Lewis has never seen him bring home a buck. In fact, he's never seen either of his cars—an enormous Ford pickup and a Mercedes SUV—with so much as a mud clod stuck in its tires. Unlike the real locals Lewis encounters in the Millburg market or on occasional visits to the tavern on the highway, Gerry isn't any more rural than Lewis, though he likes to refer to trees as "timber." He's a Portland lawyer who keeps an apartment in the Pearl District, though he does most of his work from here. He's in his early sixties, round and mostly bald, with a Van Dyke beard and a scar on his nose from a removed mole, a widower with grown children who visited with their families over the summer. During July and August, Lewis occasionally heard the screams of toddlers coming from Gerry's place, but now that the kids have gone, there's nothing but revving engines.

Though it can't be more than fifty degrees outside, the sawing has Gerry sweating hard. Before he can stop himself, Lewis thinks, *Heart attack would take care of the noise*, and then quickly chastises himself. And, as if to make him feel extra guilty, Gerry breaks into a big smile when he glances up and sees him standing there with his arms crossed. "You finally ready to take me up on the offer?" he shouts over the grind of the idling saw. "Thing's just sitting there waiting. Anytime, like I said." He switches off the motor, breathes hard. The sudden silence comes as a shock, not entirely satisfying since the sound still echoes in Lewis's head, so loud he isn't sure he'll ever be rid of it. "You want some coffee?" Gerry asks. "Come on in," he adds, waving Lewis up the cleared path—perfectly aligned pavers set with concrete mortar—to the front door.

Gerry's house can't rightly be called a cabin. A chalet, maybe, built in an outdated contemporary style with multiple skylights and a huge stone fireplace lined inside with massive composite tiles made to look like marble. Lewis hasn't been in here since the week after he closed on his place, when Gerry gave him, Veronica, and Sills a tour, talking the whole time about the plans he and his wife had had for retirement, if only she hadn't gotten sick. But how heartening it was to see a young family here, he said; it made him remember his parenting days fondly, and if they ever wanted to use the sauna, they should make themselves at home. He says it again now: "If you and your lovely wife—your daughter too. You want to take this old thing for a spin"—he opens a door beside the bathroom—"you're always welcome."

It's a gorgeous space, built with finely milled cedar, benches on three walls, a heater topped with stones to kick off steam. Gerry has turned it on with a switch out of view, and before he knows quite what he's doing, Lewis has taken off his shoes and stepped inside. He didn't realize how chilled he'd gotten standing in the river, and only now, as the warmth starts to surround him, does he shiver. He doesn't have the heart to tell Gerry he and Veronica have split, though he suspects Gerry's interest in their using the sauna isn't just about recalling his days as a young father. He saw the way Gerry glanced at Veronica's backside as he let her pass through a doorway and guesses he enjoys the idea of an attractive woman naked in his house, dripping with sweat, and then walking around in nothing but a robe. Can he blame him?

"Finished building this just before Jean's diagnosis," Gerry says from the doorway. "We got to use it one time, that's it. The camper too. Now I've got all this crap I don't need."

Lewis hasn't forgotten why he's come here, but now his anger fades as sweat beads on his forehead, and his complaints feel less urgent. "My daughter's trying to do homework," he starts, and takes a big breath of hot, cedar-scented air that cleanses his throat and lungs, clearing out what he hasn't been aware of holding in. Is that also metaphor, or is one small, hard chunk of the last year's pain really melting and washing out of his pores?

"Treasure it while you can," Gerry says before he can continue. "It don't last long."

The rural colloquialism sounds forced, as much a pose as the collection of guns in the garage, but this, too, Lewis can't hold against him. Gerry lifts a scoop from a bucket, pours water on the rocks. Then he steps out and closes the door, and Lewis leans back against the cedar boards, letting the steam fill his lungs. How long does he stay this way? Five minutes? Ten? When he finally forces himself up and opens the door, he finds Gerry still standing in the hallway, hands in pockets, staring down its length. What does he see there? The generic floral paintings hanging on the walls? The empty space where his wife should have been?

"Better head back," Lewis says. "Thanks for showing me this beauty."

"I'll be visiting the kids next month," Gerry says. "You and your girls want to use it while I'm gone, you go right ahead. I'll show you where I hide the spare key."

Lewis can feel the warmth in his cheeks as he walks back up the road and guesses they're still red when he steps inside. Sills is on her belly on the living room rug, pencil scratching across the page of an algebra workbook. As soon as he shuts the door, the sound of the leaf blower starts up again. It seems even louder now, as if it's blowing in their driveway rather than Gerry's.

"Lotta good that did."

"I bought you fifteen minutes."

"I still have twelve pages to go."

"Get your hiking boots," he says. "I'll tell your teacher you had a migraine and couldn't get it done."

"I'll finish at the lake," she says.

6. BUTTS

OUTSIDE THE BALLET STUDIO, Skye calls goodbye to her classmates and their moms as they get into their cars and drive away. Her teacher, Miss Andi, a slender redhead with an impossibly long neck, offers to wait with her, but Skye says it's no big deal, she'll be fine. "My dad'll be here any minute."

"It's cold out," Miss Andi says. "Why don't you come in while I grab my stuff?"

"I'm fine," Skye says again.

It is indeed cold for October, and drizzly, and she doesn't have a coat. Even with sweats covering her tights, the breeze makes her skin prickle. She stands under the studio's eaves and watches traffic whiz by in either direction. It's embarrassing enough to have one parent drop her off and another pick her up—she's the only girl in the class without a mom watching her practice through the big window in the waiting room—but it's worse having this huge backpack over her shoulder, with all her clothes and homework for the weekend. "Going on a trip?" one of the moms asked, and before Skye could answer, her daughter tugged her sleeve and whispered in her ear. "Have a great weekend," the mom said and hustled her daughter away, as if broken homes might be contagious.

At school, Skye knows plenty of kids with divorced parents, but not at ballet. The girls here are perfect and tidy, and so are their home lives. Most of them are aggressively Christian, wearing crosses and talking to each other about church, and their families look like something out of an old TV show, their dads always at work, their moms only in the kitchen or shopping or driving them to activities. Half of them are homeschooled. "I don't know why you keep going there," her friend June— whose parents have been split up since the first grade—asked when she described the girls who let out horrified gasps when she twisted an ankle and swore at the ceiling. "You know ballet was invented by some creepy dude who just wanted to look at underage girls' butts."

Even if she agreed, she'd never consider quitting. She loves dancing more than just about anything else, though she isn't especially talented at it, just average. Something happens to her when she's moving in rhythm to the music Miss Andi blasts from the studio's speakers, when she hears two dozen feet land at roughly the same time. She feels more in control while she's moving, and at the same time more able to let herself go, release her body into the choreography she's memorized. She has no ambition to be a great dancer, only to keep doing it for as long as she's able, even if it means standing outside in the cold waiting for her father, who finally pulls into the parking lot just as Miss Andi returns wearing a long wool coat, unbuttoned, her hair released from its bun and spilling red curls down her back and over her shoulders.

She's shivering when she gets into the car, but her father doesn't seem to notice. "Got held up at work," he says, though she can see in his cupholder a fresh take-out cappuccino from the coffee shop beside his office, still steaming. "Why aren't you wearing a jacket?"

He waves to Miss Andi, whose leotard shows through the loose neckline of a flowered dress. Miss Andi waggles fingers in return.

"Don't flirt," Skye says as he waits for an opening to pull out of the parking lot. "She's half your age."

"Waving isn't flirting," her father says.

"And she's got a boyfriend."

"She's only twenty-three?"

"Twenty-five."

"That's more than half my age."

"Can I drink some of this?" she asks, already lifting the warm cup to her mouth. She takes a sip, tastes bitter foam, then liquid hot enough to burn her tongue, but still she can't stop her teeth from chattering.

"You need to remember a jacket," her father says. "You can't expect your mom to remind you every time."

"June thinks I should quit ballet," she says when they're on the road.

"You love ballet."

"She says it's retrograde."

"Regressive?"

"Whatever." She blows in the cup lid's tiny opening, takes another sip. This time it's pleasantly hot, though still too bitter, and she sets it down. "She thinks it's humiliating for girls to have to show off their bodies to strangers."

"Is that what you think too?"

"I don't know."

"There's probably a feminist perspective. A way to see it

as empowering. Owning your body and all that. You should ask your mom what she thinks. Not like she's ever held back an opinion." He tries to laugh, but she can tell it's forced. "It's good exercise, no question about that."

"Why do guys like to look at butts anyway? I mean, it's kind of gross."

This time his laugh is genuine. She wants to join him, but she's still too cold and irritated.

"Maybe I'll quit," she says.

"I'll support you no matter what," he says. "But don't do it just because June says so. I mean, doesn't she do roller derby?"

"Yeah. So?"

"And they wear spandex and fishnets at their bouts."

"It's punk," she says.

"So she's got punk boys looking at her butt."

"And I get Christian girls' brothers."

"Maybe you should try softball. Or field hockey. Something with loose uniforms."

"I wish no one would look," she says, but that's not really true, either. She just wants to choose who looks, where, and when. And anyway, she knows those girls' brothers only look at Miss Andi's butt, which is round, tight, and muscled. "I wish guys weren't so gross."

"I hear you," her father says.

"I might really quit," she says. "After the next recital."

"You do what you need to do," he says.

"I mean, I don't see what the big deal is. With Miss Andi's. All the girls talk about how perfect it is. It's just a butt. She sits on it and poops out of it. Why does everyone have to stare at it?"

Her father reaches for the cup and takes a long sip.

7. SECRETS

HE'S BEEN WAITING ALL weekend for the phone to ring with news about the cat. Veronica sent him a text message just before he left work to pick Sills up on Friday, letting him know she was rushing Verlaine to the emergency vet. The cat had been missing for a day, which wasn't unusual—more than once he'd gotten himself stuck in a neighbor's garage—but when he reappeared that afternoon, he just hunched in the middle of the driveway, unresponsive when she called. A second text came just as he was pulling into the ballet studio's parking lot: *High fever, dehydration, stomach distended with gas. Doesn't look great.* He debated with himself whether to tell Sills and then decided to wait. *Let me know if I should bring her to see him,* he texted back, leaving it to Veronica to make the call.

And now he regrets not going to see the cat himself. Lewis was the one who first found Verlaine, half-wild and slinking around their back fence, when they moved to Salem. And Lewis was the one who named him, too, not after the French poet but after the New York guitar player who'd named himself after the poet. The name also went well with Veronica's. This was during the first year of their marriage, when he still said her name to himself all day as he went about his job or shopped for groceries or browsed in the used bookstore. Verlaine was a tough-looking tabby with a bent tail and a patch of fur missing from his back left paw, but as soon as they took him in, he adjusted to domestic life, sleeping on their bed every night, chasing a string Lewis trailed around for him, the meat around his ribs filling out on high-end kibble.

Lewis always considered Verlaine his cat, but when he moved out, he couldn't even contemplate taking him along. He wouldn't have been able to roam the yard beside the river, not without getting eaten by a coyote within days. It wouldn't have been fair to lock him inside after a whole life of rambling. And it wouldn't have been fair to Sills, either, to snatch away one last connection to the life she'd known for her first twelve years. Lewis already said his farewell to Verlaine, told himself he might never see the cat again, but only now does the possibility truly sink in.

All weekend his thoughts drift to the cat—thirteen years old now, with a hint of arthritis in his rear joints, deaf in one ear—alone in the hospital, long abandoned by the person who fed and played with him for more than a decade. He tries to maintain a cheerful front, hustling Sills out to a pumpkin patch and corn maze down in the valley even though it's already a few days after Halloween. They'll decorate for Thanksgiving, he says. Anything to keep them both busy. But his mind wanders as they search the half-empty field of squash, the vines already dried up and rotting in the furrows, and it's not long before she suspects something is wrong, though he refuses to divulge the truth even when she calls attention to his distraction.

"Fine," she says. "I don't want to know anyway."

"It's nothing," he says, pushing a wheelbarrow with a pair of enormous, misshapen pumpkins and struggling to keep it from tipping over. "Probably nothing. I'd tell you if it was something you should worry about."

"Do you have cancer or something?"

"I wouldn't keep that from you," he says, though he's not sure whether that's true. Wouldn't he want to protect her for as long as possible? What good would it do her to know if he was sick, or for that matter, for her to know Verlaine is in the hospital, if all she can do is see him in pain and say goodbye? The idea of it chokes him up once more, and he says, as he ducks into the corn maze, "Whoever makes it through first gets an extra-large hot chocolate."

He wants it to be Sills, wants to treat her in advance of any suffering that might follow. But he finds it too easy to maneuver through the maze, makes a few turns and ends up at the exit without even trying, then waits for her before stepping out in hopes that she might get competitive and try to race him to the finish line. But after another minute he gets tired of standing, leaves the maze, and sits on a hay bale to wait. She takes a few more minutes to wander out without any sign of urgency or enthusiasm.

"Guess you're stuck watching me drink," he says. "Lucky for you, I like sharing."

She shrugs, strolls past him. "You're not the only one with a secret," she says.

"Oh? And I suppose you think I'll want to know badly enough to tell you mine?"

"It doesn't matter if you did. I still wouldn't tell."

There's no malice in her voice as she says it, nothing manipulative, even, just the certainty of a decision definitively made. "I'm glad you have secrets. You should. I don't want to know."

"Good. I don't want to know yours either."

"It's not really a secret anyway," he says, pushing the wheelbarrow again, the pumpkins jostling against each other as he rolls over a rut in the muddy grass. "Just something I'm a little concerned about. But I don't want you to have to worry."

"Mine's a real secret," she says. "But I'm keeping it."

By then they've reached the food stand beside the barn, and though he knows he'd be better off with apple cider, he orders hot chocolate and says, "You can have one too. Even if you didn't try in the maze."

She orders and then says, "I still won't tell you. Even if you try to bribe me."

"I wasn't. You don't have to. I don't want you to."

They sip without speaking. Until recently, whenever she got hot chocolate, Sills would come away with her face covered in whipped cream. Even now she has trouble not getting some on her nose, though she quickly wipes it off and looks around furtively, as if checking to see who might have noticed. "There's still a spot on your chin," he says, but she smacks his hand away when he tries to clean it with his thumb.

On the drive back to the cabin, he can't take it anymore. He tells her about Verlaine. She shrugs again. "I know."

"You do?"

"Mom texted me too."

"Aren't you worried about him?"

"Sure. But it's not like I could do anything about it if I were there. She can't even go in and see him."

"What if . . .? I mean—"

"He's not going to die," she says firmly and looks out the passenger window. "She'll call us if we need to come."

"Now you better say yours."

"No chance."

"What do you mean?"

"I'm never telling."

"That's not fair."

"You didn't have to tell. You just have no willpower."

"Fine," he says. "I don't want to know anyway."

When they get back to the cabin, the landline phone is blinking to indicate there's a voice mail. They both stare at it. "Shouldn't you listen to the message?" Sills asks.

"Maybe you ought to do it. I haven't seen him in months. He's really your cat now."

"I think you should."

"Okay," he says and approaches the phone. "I will. If you tell me yours."

She turns and heads out back with her book. The light on the receiver blinks and blinks, but he can't bring himself to pick it up. It can keep its secrets, too, for now. After a few minutes he grabs a magazine and joins her on the deck. They lounge in the brisk air, reading in silence.

8. PLAN D

FOR THE PAST THREE weeks, her father has been building
something in the backyard. She thinks of it as *something* because
what it's supposed to be has changed several times during the
construction. At first it was going to be a stand-alone woodshed,
tall enough to walk into and raise your arms over your head;
then a lean-to against the existing garden shed, which was here
when they first bought the place; and now a wooden box about
six feet long and three feet wide—like a coffin, only with a lid
that's supposed to slant to slough off the rain. But he hasn't put
the hinges on level, and when he lowers it, one side sticks open
six inches, welcoming the water it's meant to keep out. She sees
him out there swearing to himself as he runs the drill in reverse
to pull out the screws, stripping one in the process and kicking
a corner of the box. Her mother has always been the handier
one; she installed the cabinets in their Salem bathroom, hung
shelves in her office, discovered a pocket in the wall beside
Skye's closet and built her a secret room with a half-sized door
where she kept her stuffed animals when she was younger, and

then her spells and potions during the brief period she wanted to be a witch, and now the magazines her mother tells her are "anti-feminist" and "reactionary," though she still likes to look at the pictures and read articles about fashion and beauty and cute hairstyles even if she doesn't want to bother getting them herself.

Her father had been a helper on these projects, the one who held things still, who provided some extra resistance when necessary, but he has no precision, no comfort with power tools. He's told her it's because both his parents grew up in rented city apartments, where they'd call the super if anything needed fixing. His own father never taught him anything practical, except maybe how to balance a checkbook—which he never does—and tie a knot in fishing line. Now he's bought himself some of the tools he needs and borrowed others from their neighbor Gerry, but he's still at a loss when it comes to making anything level. So she puts on her rain gear—she's forgotten her jacket again, but he bought her a plastic poncho at a gas station on their way out of town—steps across the muddy yard, and asks if she can help.

"You can push against this side to give me some leverage," he says. She can tell he's grateful, though he won't admit it. He's trying to project calm and control, though she knows he's fuming. She holds the lid and braces her shoulder against the opposite side while he runs the drill again. The next screw strips, too, and she smells smoke. "God damn it," he whispers.

"Maybe you need a break," Skye says. "I'll make some hot chocolate."

"I've got to get this done," he says. "All that wood's gonna be useless if I don't get it in soon."

She knew he bought too much firewood as soon as he

ordered it. She heard him on the phone with the person who delivered: two cords, he'd said, though last year he'd gotten two yards. "It was definitely two cords," he told her, though she remembered clearly, because she'd imagined two yards meant two backyards' worth and then was disappointed to see only a table-size pile easily covered by a tarp. Now there's four times that amount sitting beside the deck, and the tarp covers less than half; the rest has been getting soaked most days since mid-October.

"Whenever Mom strips them, she uses another bit to drill off the top."

"That's what I was planning to do next," he says and flips open the case of bits Gerry lent him.

"A bigger one," she says when he starts to clamp on one slightly narrower than the screw head.

He does what she says, and then comes the smell of metal sparking on metal, along with that of sap bleeding from fresh plywood. The hinge comes free. She uses a pair of pliers to pull out the remaining pieces of screw. Then he's ready to go at it again, make new holes by eyeballing, but she stops him, pulls out a tape measure, makes pencil marks on the wood. Rain drips down his face, making him look even more helpless. "If I had to do high school over again, I'd definitely take woodshop," he says. Then he shudders, pushes his wet hair back from his forehead. "Thank the gods I don't have to. Once in a lifetime of that torture is plenty." Then he pauses, shrugs, says, "I'm sure it'll be much better for you. It's not the 1980s. Or New Jersey."

"I'll hold," she says. "You drill."

It takes them another half hour, maybe forty-five minutes, and then the lid is on. It closes, and the gap is only an inch wide. "Good enough," her father says. "I can cover that with a piece of trim. Or a plastic bag. Something to worry about another day. Let's get the wood in."

They both grab an armful of logs—none of which he's split yet—and carry them to the box. She drops hers in first, and when they hit the bottom, a small cloud of sawdust bursts out, and little orange-brown bugs scatter into the corners. "Uh, Dad?"

He lets out a long breath and then a sad little laugh. "Right."

"Termites?"

"Plan B." He glances at the huge pile of wood, some of it resting against the fir posts holding up the deck. "I guess we've already gone through B. This was C. So. On to D, right?"

They spend the rest of the afternoon moving the pile away from the deck to the back of the yard, where it can get safely chewed and rot for the next twenty years. Later, after he showers, and while she's drinking her second cup of hot chocolate, she hears him on the phone. "That's right. Two yards. I'll get more later if I need it."

9. HOARDER

When he first started coming to the river, Lewis would take the canyon road slowly, always braking on its tight curves, and it would irritate him whenever someone came up fast from behind, riding his tail to urge him to hit the gas or pull onto the shoulder. Now, though, after driving it twice a day for most of a year, it makes him wild with impatience to get stuck behind someone who won't go over fifty on the straightaways and slows to thirty-five on the curves signed to be taken at twenty-five. He can't help rolling up close, tapping his thumbs on the steering wheel, as if the few extra minutes on the road will rob him of crucial time he might spend at home. Today he's behind a small orange pickup from the '70s, hardly big enough to call a pickup, though its bed is crammed with furniture and boxes partially tied down with a tarp whose loose corner flaps tauntingly in front of his windshield.

"Why don't you give him some space," Sills says when the truck slows to cross the first bridge, nearly coming to a stop to take a dip on the far side. Lewis's bumper is inches away, and it takes all his restraint to keep from giving a little nudge.

"I'm trying to get you home for dinner," he says. "You're probably starving."

"I ate a string cheese before practice."

"That ought to hold you for days."

"What's for dinner, anyway?"

"We'll have to see what's in the fridge."

"Did you go shopping this week?"

"I'll go tomorrow."

By now he's eased back from the truck, keeping at least fifty feet between them, though it literally pains him not to let his foot down on the gas pedal—the awkward angle makes his foot twinge with the start of a cramp. There's no one behind him and nothing particularly important waiting for them at home. He should just enjoy this time alone with his daughter, and so he tries to ask questions about her week—*how was school, how was ballet, did she sort out the drama with her friends*—all of which she answers with a single word before going silent while the stupid truck putters along in front of him, and he fills with enough rage to ram it. But then its left turn signal begins blinking, the bulb bare because its casing has broken off, and after another quarter mile it turns up a long dirt driveway he's passed hundreds of times without ever seeing anyone on it. It leads to an old farmhouse, the last before the road begins to climb and the forest closes in. Here are some open fields, a few white oaks, a tumbledown barn, a pair of goats behind a split-log fence, and a donkey behind another. Out front is a handwritten sign on a wooden board, one they've seen every week but never heeded:

Firewood $5

Eggs $5

Peace of mind free

Lewis and Sills look at each other at the same moment. He knows they're both thinking the same thing. "Why not?" he says. "Omelets for dinner."

"We could use some firewood too," she says.

"We've got plenty."

"It's all wet and gross and full of bugs, and you never want to go out and get it."

"The new delivery should come Sunday."

"That doesn't help us tonight."

"Omelets and a fire," he says.

"And I could use some peace," she says.

"I'm guessing he means *piece*. With an *i* and *e*."

"What's the difference?"

"Depends which piece he gives us."

The truck bounces down the muddy track ahead of them. The deeper into the yard they go, the more junk they spy in the tall grass: rusted tractors, rotting wooden crates, a rowboat full of bald tires. By the time they reach the house, the pickup's owner has begun unloading the bed, carrying metal folding chairs three at a time to the front porch, which is already crammed with objects: standing lamps, wicker tables, laminate bookshelves, a pair of clawfoot tubs, cardboard boxes stacked five high. He's an old guy with a cap pulled low on his forehead, so many wrinkles around his mouth, and so deep, it's hard to distinguish his lips.

"We're in the market for some eggs," Lewis calls, chagrined to hear himself adopting a vaguely country accent, as he always does when speaking to locals—out of insecurity or condescension or both, he isn't sure. "If you got any right now."

"Sign says I do," the old guy says, lifting another pair of chairs from the truck bed.

"Nothing better than fresh," Lewis says. "What kind of chickens are they?"

One of his Portland friends used to raise chickens in his backyard, and he'd always go on about the breeds: Ameraucanas, which lay blue eggs; black copper Marans, dark brown. None of those chickens are still around. Some got eaten by raccoons; the others his friend sold off after he got tired of cleaning their coop.

"Brown ones," the old guy says. Lewis knows Sills must be smirking behind him, but he doesn't turn to look.

She says, "What do you do with all that stuff?"

"Mind my own business with it," the old guy says.

"I mean, are you going to fix it up and sell it?"

"You see anything you like?"

"We'll take two dozen eggs," Lewis says. "And a couple bundles of firewood too."

"Big spender," the old guy says.

Sills is already up on the porch, the feet of her ballet tights flapping at her ankles as she leans over an old couch to get a look at something on the other side.

"Can I give you a hand with those?" Lewis asks as the old guy drags the last of the folding chairs up the steps and shoves them into a tight space between the railing and a dresser with feet in the shape of hooves.

"Maybe if you asked before I finished," the old guy says.

"I totally want this," Sills says and pulls up what Lewis thinks at first is a stuffed beaver mounted on a wooden stand, until he sees that its tail is the wrong shape, and its teeth are too small, and it generally looks like a fat squirrel. Yellow-bellied marmot, most likely, or maybe just an ordinary groundhog.

"That's historic," the old guy says. "Trapped in the 1880s."

"How do you know?" Sills asks.

"I do my research," the old guy says.

"Didn't they trap for fur? Why mount it?"

"This one's got a summer pelt. Not warm enough to make a hat."

Sills turns it over and reads something on the base. "Says ten dollars and ninety-nine cents. Is that what you're selling it for? Or what you paid for it?"

"It's worth six times that much," the old guy says.

"We'll take the firewood and the eggs," Lewis says, holding out a twenty-dollar bill.

"We'll give you fifteen for the rat," Sills says.

"No, we won't," Lewis says.

"I've got my own money," Sills says.

"It's priceless," the old guy says.

"Twenty," Sills says, running her hand down the marmot's head and neck.

"Forget it, little lady," the old guy says. "It's not for sale."

"Two dozen eggs, and we'll be on our way," Lewis says.

When they're back in the car, Sills says, sadly, "He's gonna keep piling it up. That rat'll be staring down at him when he dies under all that junk."

"Yup," Lewis says.

"I just wanted to help him."

"Some people you can't help."

"Those eggs are rotten," she says.

"I know."

"What are we gonna eat?"

"There's some chicken nuggets in the freezer. Don't worry, they're not too old. We'll be fine."

10. MAFIA

ONE WEEKEND IN LATE November, her friend Lizzy comes to stay at the river. Skye has been looking forward to the visit for weeks, talking through the details with her father, even mentioning it to her mother, who asks, "You sure your dad can handle two of you? Did you remind him to pick up extra food? Did you find out if she has any allergies?"

Lizzy is her best friend, though she's never said so out loud. She thinks she's Lizzy's best friend, too, but it's an unspoken rule of their friend group not to talk about bests, for fear of hurting feelings and splintering into pairs. Lizzy has said that she thinks of herself as a tabletop and that her friends are the legs holding her up—she needs at least four, or she'll get off-balance. With only one, she'd topple for sure. So Skye holds back when they're with the group, tries to keep from seeming too eager, avoids talking about books she and Lizzy have both read or movies they've both seen that the others haven't. But now she'll have Lizzy to herself for two days and three nights, and how can they not return on Monday closer than ever, with inside jokes and stories that will be theirs alone? They won't have to acknowledge that they're better friends than any of the others—it will go without saying.

They pick her up on Friday night from her house in South Salem, a huge place with white brick on the front, lights lining the path from the street like a runway, a garage the size of the cabin. Her parents both come onto the front steps to see her off, even though it's cold outside and raining. They're tall and slender like her, well-dressed even at home. They both give her long hugs. She's wheeling a little suitcase, the kind you take on airplanes. Skye's father rolls down his window, waves to her parents, calls, "We'll take good care of her." Skye moves to the back seat so they can sit together, but Lizzy misunderstands, thinks she wants her to take the front. She settles next to Skye's father, says, "Thanks so much for having me, Mr. Nelson," and her father makes small talk with her on the way up the canyon. Skye, not used to sitting in the back, fights off car sickness the whole time, the seat belt cutting into her shoulder as each curve sends her toppling to the side.

When they arrive, Lizzy lets her father carry her suitcase inside. "It's so cute!" she exclaims, though there's unease in her voice, and she doesn't look at Skye when she says it. Is it smaller than she imagined? Darker? Farther out in the middle of nowhere? Unlike their friend June, who claims to hate the outdoors—"Trees freak me out," she's said—Lizzy talks all the time about the camping trips she and her family take in the summer, the remote places they visit in Eastern Oregon where they've encountered rattlesnakes near their tents. She's not generally prissy like the girls in Skye's ballet class—she's cut her hair short and wears temporary tattoos of anime characters on her arms—but now she checks every corner, as if she expects something to jump out at her. In Skye's bedroom, she says,

"Can we really both fit in here?" to which her father responds, "You two can have the loft if you want. I'll take the couch."

And Lizzy: "Thanks so much, Mr. Nelson."

Skye imagined the two of them in her small room, sharing the bed and whispering all night. The loft has no door. The bed is bigger, but Lizzy asks for a sleeping bag so she can stretch out on the rug instead. When her father brings it up, once again: "Thanks, Mr. Nelson."

It's this way all weekend: Mr. Nelson this, Mr. Nelson that. Did her parents tell her she needed to be polite at every second? Did they warn her to stay on the good side of the strange, divorced man who lives alone in the woods? The first night Lizzy says she's exhausted soon after dinner and falls asleep right away. The next morning she's up early, already down-stairs and dressed when Skye wakes, standing in the kitchen while her father scrambles eggs. "You girls go have fun," he says after they've eaten, but Lizzy insists on helping with the dishes, and then she wants him to come with them to the river. Later she says he has to join them in their game of Uno because it's boring with just two people. Skye gets no time with her alone, and she realizes this is how Lizzy wants it—no chance for one leg to grow longer and thicker and upset the balance of her table. Or something like that. Skye wonders if she's been wrong to think of Lizzy as her best friend—or if she's really her friend at all.

On their last night, Lizzy suggests they play Mafia, a game she invented, Skye is pretty sure, though she said she learned it from one of her cousins. They play it at lunch among their group of friends—another way to keep them all on the same page, keep them from arguing about TV shows they do or don't like, or boys they think are or aren't cute, or which they're sure are or aren't gay. "I don't think Dad would like it," Skye says, but her father, clueless, smiles and answers, "I'll give it a try."

The game, which makes sense when she's playing it with her friends, now seems bizarre to her, maybe even a little stupid when her father's involved. The rules are simple enough: they each get a slip of paper informing them of their role, and they have to provide clues but try to keep each other from guessing for as long as possible. One of them is a mafia hit woman (or man), one of them is the victim, one of them is a cop; if they have more people playing, another would be a snitch, and a fifth might be the godmother (or father). When they play at school, they all laugh a lot and talk in funny voices and make wisecracks, and when they discover the killer, they all shout accusations and chase each other around the monkey bars.

But tonight the game is quiet and serious, and her father is too invested in winning. His brows bunch, his eyes cut left and right. Everything about this is wrong. It's as if the game has transformed into something different because they're playing it in the cabin, or else Lizzy has turned into a different person when she's away from their other friends. She keeps glancing at Skye's father, as if she's only concerned that he's enjoying himself and doesn't care at all that Skye is miserable—the victim, murdered by one of these two people she's trusted, who ask each other terse questions to find the guilty party. It's pretty quickly clear that Lizzy is mafia, that she's killed her in cold blood, but her father still seems unsure. She understands without being told, however, that she's supposed to let him guess correctly. He does, eventually, but instead of condemning Lizzy for her actions and putting her in jail as they would on the playground, he says in a garbled Italian accent, "I think she deserved it. For betraying the family code."

Later, when they're getting ready for bed, Skye says, "I thought the game was only for us. You know, our friend group."

"I play it with my parents and brother all the time," Lizzy says. "Otherwise, we don't have anything to talk about."

She seems not to have anything to talk about with Skye now, either, and the two of them lie in darkness, both awake, Skye is sure, listening to rain pelting the roof. She tries to remember what it was like when her parents were still together and the three of them would sit around after dinner. Would they still be together if they'd played Mafia in the evenings? She's grateful to have things to talk about with her mom when the two of them are on their own, and with her dad, too, most of the time—and if they don't have anything to say, the silence isn't usually so excruciating that she'd pretend to fall asleep, as she does now, making what she hopes are realistic sounds of heavy breathing with the occasional hint of a snore. Real sleep doesn't come for a long time.

The next day, when her father drops them off at school, Lizzy is full of thanks for Mr. Nelson and then runs up the steps to the building, wheeling her suitcase behind her without waiting for Skye. "Nice kid," her father says as she moves from the back seat to the front.

"I think I like it better there when it's just the two of us," she says.

"I won't argue with that," he says.

"Mafia's a stupid game."

"Next weekend we'll play Texas Hold'em," he says. "Your allowance against my savings. Which are just about the same."

She leans across the seat, gives him a quick hug, and hurries up the steps. On her way inside, June, wearing all black as usual and with newly painted black fingernails, catches up to her and asks, "You and Liz sisters now?"

"Would have been more fun if you were there," Skye says.

"No way you're getting me to spend a weekend around all those trees."

"We're a family," Skye says. "Better all together."

"Mafia family," June says. "Ready to stab each other in the back."

11. EMISSIONS

SHE'S BEEN GLOWERING AT him all weekend, hardly answering when he speaks. He doesn't know what he's done wrong— he's gone over a list of potential offenses in his mind and can't pinpoint anything—but gives her space anyway, letting her spend the days reading, doing homework, and listening to music on headphones. More than once he's stopped himself from suggesting she come outside, get some fresh air, tell him what's bothering her. The rain doesn't let up much, but he spends a few hours in it anyway, splitting and stacking some wood, raking fallen fir needles from the shed roof so they won't rot the plywood beneath the asphalt shingles.

He's tired of her accusatory glare, tired of feeling con-stantly judged by a not-quite-thirteen-year-old who can never remember to bring her rain jacket home from school and then complains when her sweatshirt soaks through on a three-minute walk. He's done so much for her, has stepped up in a way he wasn't sure he could, has gotten himself on track with most of his bills, has remembered to keep the refrigerator stocked with things she likes, has dedicated himself to being a good parent—he who told all the women he'd dated before meeting Veronica that he didn't want children—and yet she doesn't appreciate a bit of it, doesn't thank him for anything. He works himself into a state of outrage as he swings the maul, enjoying the burn in his arms and the thunk of metal in wood, and also finds amusement in this image of himself splitting logs in the rain: little New Jersey Jew playing man of the mountains.

When he goes inside, sweating, she gives him that frown again, even more bitter than before, the big headphones covering her ears making her look like some cyborg out of the B movies he loved as a teenager. She's sitting cross-legged on the floor with a spiral notebook open in her lap, a folder and schoolbooks spread around her. "What?" he says. "What'd I do?"

She squints at him, deaf from whatever music is blasting straight into her brain. "What?" she answers but doesn't take the headphones off, so he goes to the sink to warm his hands under hot water. The skin on either side of his joints is red and sore. He hasn't done enough work yet to form calluses, and now his fingers ache, whether from cold or exertion he doesn't know. "What?" she calls again. When he turns back, she has the headphones around her neck, but she's shouting as if there's still music drowning out her words. "What do you want?"

"I asked you what," he says. "You keep scowling at me. What'd I do wrong? Aside from ruining your whole life and everything, making you spend every weekend in these boring, ugly old woods."

"Not just my life," she says, the rims of her eyes reddening, her voice going nasal. "Everyone's. You ruined the whole planet."

"Me?"

"You and your whole stupid, selfish generation."

"You're thinking about the baby boomers," he says. "You know, Bubby and Papa and all their golf-playing friends. I'm Gen X. We've tried—"

"Look at this," she says and holds up a photo clipped from a magazine. He's too far away to glimpse more than white shapes on a blue field. "You did this."

When he steps closer, he sees: an emaciated polar bear standing on a chunk of ice floating in open water. He's come across the image before, or others like it, and it always has the effect of inducing sadness that quickly tips toward despair and resignation. *We're fucked*, he thinks, and wants to go back to the river and enjoy what's there while he can.

"I donate to the Nature Conservancy every year," he says. "And the national resources thing. Defense council? I was even a member of Greenpeace when I was in college. What are you talking about?"

"Your car," she says. "You drive what, a hundred miles every day?"

"Not quite."

"And fill up your tank twice a week?"

"It gets thirty miles a gallon."

"It's not even a hybrid," she says.

And then he learns: she's supposed to write a paper about how she and her family contribute to climate change, how they can work to reduce their carbon footprint. He's had his car for a dozen years, bought used soon after Sills was born. He'd traded his beat-to-shit Nova for the CR-V because it was safer. At the time, he thought of it as ridiculously suburban, as close to the station wagons of his childhood as you could get without buying a minivan. But like most things, what he once swore off he later learned to accommodate in changing circumstances. What he really meant when he'd told those women he'd dated that he didn't want children was that he didn't want to have children with them. Within weeks of meeting Veronica and falling in love, he'd thought, *I'd raise chickens with this woman, or goats, or rhinoceri.* "I think kids are great," he told her when she made it clear she intended to have a family and wouldn't waste time with someone who didn't.

He has come to love his CR-V, to consider it a second home. It gets him to fishing holes and trailheads: places, to his surprise, he has come to value so much more than the raucous music clubs to which he drove the Nova—and from which he often emerged too drunk to drive it home, opting instead for a cab and riding the bus hungover the next morning to retrieve it. He can't imagine giving up the car, nor can he afford to replace it with anything more efficient. But neither does he want to call Sills's attention to things he could easily change, such as using the woodstove, which he doesn't need for heat—the electric heat pump gives them all they need—and enjoys instead for purely aesthetic reasons: he can spend hours watching flames dance across the top of a split log, the rhythmic movement of combustion producing light, nothing else like it.

"I've got to get to work, don't I?" he says. "I hardly drive at all on weekends. Not like a lot of people, who road-trip to watch college football games or something."

"They're going extinct," she says, quieter now, with a hopelessness far more unnerving than her anger. "By the time I'm your age, they'll all be gone."

"If electric cars weren't so damn expensive," he says. "If our spineless legislators weren't in the pocket of the oil companies.

I mean, they could put resources toward what matters instead of paying for billion-dollar warplanes—"

"You could save up," she says. "Start putting away a little every month."

"I can do that," he says. "Sure. I will."

"And switch out the lightbulbs for better ones."

"Fluorescent? They give me headaches."

"These are making all the ice melt."

"I hear there are some decent LEDs on the market. I'll give those a try."

"I don't want to live in a world without polar bears," she says.

"You should talk to your mom about her gas stove," he says before he can stop himself. "And the furnace too."

By then she's put the headphones back on and is furiously scribbling in her notebook. He's relieved, at least, that her seething look is no longer trained on him. Later, when she's in bed, he reads what she wrote and learns that he's going to buy a new car—an electric one, or at least a hybrid—by the end of next year.

12. TRUST

ONE EVENING, WHEN THE rain hasn't let up for days and they've both grown restless, her father grimacing as he stands, then rolling shoulders and kneading a knot in his neck, Skye offers to teach him some yoga poses. She's been taking a class once a week with her mom and has been badgering him to try it. Why suffer all the time? Why not take care of yourself when all it requires is half an hour a day? Now, to her surprise, he agrees, even seems to welcome the idea. He encourages her further by groaning melodramatically as he crouches into child's pose. They both laugh when they compare their standing forward bend, Skye putting both hands flat on the floor, her father unable to reach his shins.

"This one's my favorite," he says when she lets him lie flat on his back in Shavasana.

"You're a corpse," she says, "so stop talking." Then she hears only the uneven stutter of air in his lungs. "Only you're a corpse that needs to pay attention to your breath. In through the nose, out through the mouth." He manages it correctly for a few breaths, then dozes off and wakes himself with a snort.

Afterward, she pulls chairs away from the dining table, scatters them around the front room, tells him to close his eyes. He does. "Put out your finger," she says, and he does that, too. She links her own finger with his and tugs. He resists. "Come on," she says and explains that it's an exercise her instructor leads at the end of every class. She tugs again, and this time he follows, slowly, shuffling his feet on the rug.

"What's this have to do with yoga?" he asks.

"It's about freeing your mind. Letting go."

"My mind isn't free," he says. "It's focused on not walking into a chair."

"You've got to trust," she says. "That's the whole point."

She pulls him to the left, and when his knee grazes the couch, he opens his eyes halfway. "Remember my back," he says. "If I fall, I might not get up again."

"No peeking," she says. "Or I'll have to blindfold you."

"I feel like I'm walking the plank."

"That's good," she says. "Picture sharks below. If you don't follow me exactly, you're lunch."

She pulls harder, and he lets himself take longer strides. They turn figure eights around the chairs, his foot occasionally bumping one of the legs, but now he manages to keep his eyes closed. In class, she's always loved the feeling of being guided around the room, of abandoning herself to someone else's sight, and she's glad to give him the experience too. He'll soon start to become conscious of sounds—the rain on the roof; the clicking of his knees; Skye's breath, still phlegmy from a recent cold—and then his mind will drift further. In another minute he won't even remember he's walking around obstacles, that anything might stand in his way.

Lately, her own thoughts during the exercise have meandered to a boy in school. She hadn't really noticed him until he was assigned to play the judge in a mock trial they'd been acting out. A way to learn about the legal system, her teacher said, though if Skye, who'd played a juror, learned anything other than how excruciatingly dull the legal system was, how little she cared about whether the defendant had broken this or that statute, she couldn't have said what, except that the judge—Trayton Bush—was funnier than she'd realized, and cuter, with long eyelashes and a fan of soft bangs that swept across his forehead.

She thinks of him again now and immediately afterward imagines her father's thoughts tracing similar paths. Not picturing a boy, of course. Who, then? Maybe an assistant in his office. Or a barista at the coffee shop where he often stops on his way home from work; she saw a fresh cup in his car when he picked her up, late again, from ballet on Friday afternoon. One of those recent college graduates she's always admired, with long arms and plucked eyebrows and a tattoo of a bird on her ankle. A woman, that is, other than her mother. The idea is so astonishing that she forgets for a moment she's supposed to be watching out for him. She leads him around the last chair too fast, and he doesn't turn with her. His eyes are closed, lightly, his face relaxed as he heads straight for the bookshelf. She pulls hard, but it's too late. His nose hits first, then mouth and chin, and finally forehead, the raw wood corner striking right between his eyes. He bounces back in such a comical way Skye can't stop herself from letting out a horrified hoot of laughter.

"It's not funny," he says and yanks his finger from her. He touches his lip and comes away with a spot of blood.

"Why didn't you follow me?"

"You walked me right into the shelf."

"I pulled this way. You kept going straight."

"I never would have done that to you," he says and goes to the bathroom, where he splashes water onto his lip and dabs it with a towel.

"You don't think I did it on purpose, do you?"

There's a red mark on his forehead, and along with the bags under his eyes and the gray hair on his temples, it makes him look older than forty-six, and tired. What barista would give him a second glance?

"I didn't," she says. "I swear."

"Do you mind?" he says and lifts the toilet seat. "I need a minute."

"We can do it again," she says.

"I don't think so."

"You can do me this time."

"No more yoga for today," he says. "A little privacy, please."

"I'll get you some ice," she calls through the closed door. "It'll keep the swelling down, okay?" When he doesn't answer, she pounds the wood with her fist. "Okay?"

13. THE ROTTEN TOOTH

THERE ARE HALF A dozen Christmas tree farms within twenty minutes of the cabin, but Sills insists on driving an hour to the one they've frequented for as long as she can remember, on a hillside north of Silver Falls. He wants to stop at the park on the way because a recent dusting of snow covers the ground and icicles hang from a few tree branches and he knows the waterfalls will be their most lovely today, but Sills is too excited to pause. She wants him to drive fast where the highway winds through the park and is nearly bouncing in her seat when they pull onto the long gravel drive between rows of perfectly shaped noble firs.

He's participated in this ritual since before she was born, but he's never enjoyed it, except for the pleasure it has given the people he loves. Veronica grew up outside of Portland and spent her childhood driving to a farm like this one and dragging a tree taller than a full-grown adult into the house, where it would shed needles all over the floor for a month before her father tossed it out back to brown all winter and spring, eventually hacking it into pieces and adding it to the woodpile to burn the following winter. Lewis had done the same thing at the house in Salem, except the last time, before cutting it up, he discovered that a pair of towhees had built a nest in the dead tree where it leaned against the silvered cedar fence. Sills found this exciting, too, until Verlaine, too old and slow to catch full-grown birds—at least healthy ones—slaughtered the hatchlings as soon as they started peeping in the branches.

Lewis, of course, never had Christmas trees growing up. His family wasn't terribly observant, and by the time he was Sills's age, they'd light Hanukkah candles for a night or two before forgetting the remainder of the eight. His parents would disperse all presents on the first night and be done with it. There were plenty of Jews in that part of northern New Jersey—especially compared to Oregon—but his neighborhood was mostly Italian and Irish Catholic, and by a week after Thanksgiving, almost every house around them would be covered in colored lights, their baubled trees displayed prominently in bay windows. Lewis's parents took their holiday asceticism as a mark of distinction, maybe even pride. They wouldn't even turn on the porch light during the month of December, and when you drove down the street their house stood out like a rotten tooth in an otherwise gleaming jaw.

But it isn't Jewish guilt or the creeping ubiquity of Christianity as a cultural default—his parents' greatest fear—that so unnerves him about the Christmas tree ritual. Rather, he just finds it senseless to cut down a perfectly healthy tree, especially to use as a symbol of some divine birth. Or worse, if you celebrated the holiday in its original pagan spirit, as Veronica did, and viewed the tree as a symbol of life's continuity in the midst of winter's darkness. If Christmas were about the human domination of nature, sure, then why not cut down a few million trees and stick one in your living room. But he prefers trees in the ground, especially the kind that would grow to seventy feet tall if you'd let them. The topiary pruning, too, offends his sensibility—it's too mannered, too unnatural to make rigid cones out of life forms that have perfectly beautiful shapes if left alone.

He hoped by this age Sills would outgrow her enthusiasm for Christmas trees—if not for Christmas itself—but if anything, her fervor has only grown this year. He understands: in the midst of loss, she needs something to celebrate, something to look forward to, and he tries to set aside his own misgivings in favor of her need as she bounds out of the car and runs into the grid of trees. They've come downhill far enough that there's no longer any snow, just mud, reddish-brown and slick. She slides and catches herself before falling. Lewis exchanges words with one of the farm's employees, who tells him what he already knows: fifty bucks each up to six feet, then sixty above. When they find one they want, they can call for someone to cut it with a chainsaw, or they can use one of the bow saws hanging on the barn door.

Sills is already calling to him: "Dad, check this one out! It's taller than you!" Before he reaches her, she's already moved on to another one. "This one's so cute. Don't you love its shape? The little twisty part at the top?" He knew, long before they arrived, that this process would take far more time than he wants to give it. When Veronica was with them, she'd eventually cut things short, saying, "That's it, we've chosen." She has a remarkable ability to close herself off to Sills's whining, as if she can't even hear it when she's no longer interested. Not so for Lewis, who'd feel it under his skin if he covered his ears, vibrating in his bones. He's prepared to go along with the search for as long as it takes to avoid complaints, but now he regrets agreeing to pick up two trees while they're here—one for the cabin, one for the Salem house, the latter of which he'll deliver to Veronica on Monday morning. To his surprise, Veronica had no qualms with this plan. "I'm too busy to take her during the week," she said on the phone. "Just don't let her get one so tall it'll leave sap on the ceiling."

Now he says, "Maybe we should just get one. It's not like you'll be at the cabin for Christmas anyway. You won't even see it much."

"I'll see it six days if we keep it till New Year's," she says, which suggests she's already thought this through at length. "Three weekends. And one is just two days before Christmas. Eve's eve."

"We don't even have any ornaments," he says and pictures the boxes in Veronica's basement, filled with glass balls and hand-painted wooden birds, things passed down from grand-parents and great-grandparents. She bought new ones each year of their marriage, too, one for each of them—ceramic icicles, felt animals, Day of the Dead skulls—and that part of the ritual Lewis did enjoy, each of them jockeying for space to hang their favorites, then remembering to hang the fragile ones higher so Verlaine wouldn't knock them down and shatter them on the wood floor. "Or any lights."

"Ours is going to be all-natural," Sills says, again with the certainty of someone who has been harboring detailed plans for weeks. "We'll make garlands out of pine cones. And use that long, stringy lichen. And the star's going to be the geode we found last year."

Unlike her, he has given his objections little thought and so has nothing prepared with which to counter her. So he stays quiet. The farm is six acres, and they walk every inch of it, or so it seems; his boot treads are clogged with mud, clumps of it hanging on the hems of his jeans. Finally they circle back to their original spot, and Sills points to the first tree she noticed. "This is it," she says. "Best of the bunch."

It is indeed a lovely tree, about seven feet tall, wide at the base, its trunk six inches across near the ground. She won't hear of them using a chainsaw or having someone else cut it for them, so he goes to the barn and fetches one of the bow saws. The first notch makes him a little sick. How can they just harvest this magnificent thing as if it's a head of lettuce or a stalk of broccoli? It would outlive all of them if left on its own. He's surprised Sills doesn't find anything sad about cutting it down. When they were in the woods, she expressed such reverence for trees. If they pass through a clear-cut, she curses people for mistreating the natural world and blames all adults for the devastation global warming will bring. But now she takes the saw from him eagerly, grinds it back and forth in the groove he's started, pushes and pulls until her arms start to burn. When he takes over, his back quickly aches from crouching, and he has to go down on his knees in the mud, cold dampness quickly seeping through to his skin. He saws and saws, and finally he's all the way through. Sills eases the tree down on its side and shouts, with sinister glee, "You're ours now!"

Before he can catch his breath, she's already darted over to a second one, a little narrower than the first, not quite as tall, not as well pruned. "This one for the cabin," she says, and he's surprised to find himself disappointed that he gets the lesser of the two.

"You sure you want to take down another one?" he asks. "I mean, once you cut them, they're gone. They won't grow back."

She looks at him strangely for a long moment, a hint of disgust dipping the edges of her mouth. "They'll cut it eventually," she says. "It's not like they're gonna let a forest grow in the middle of their farm."

He knows that; of course he does. But somehow it's different being the one to do the cutting. He crouches, feels a sharp twinge in his lower back, winces.

"Let me do it," she says, but she can't manage to get the teeth to catch, just mangles the bark near the ground. Her troubled expression deepens.

"I've got it," he says.

This time he keeps sawing without stopping, without letting her take a turn. Sawdust spits from either side of the trunk, sap leaks onto the blade. His arms ache, and he's sweating, but he doesn't let up. If anyone's going to do the killing, it should be him, in case she might one day feel regret. This time he forgets to warn her when he's coming to the end, and the tree falls over before she can grab it, leaving some long splinters on one side of the trunk and bending a few branches in the mud.

She's silent as he ties the trees to the top of the car—angry, he's sure, because he made her think about something she'd prefer to ignore. But he's only somewhat sorry to have sullied a custom she loves. She's also a Jew after all—in the eyes of Nazis, at least, if not the Orthodox. Shouldn't she have some sense of the world as flawed and compromised, even in its joyful moments?

By the time they reach the falls, all the snow has melted. He drives past without stopping.

WINTER

14. TRESPASSING

HE'S BEEN TALKING ABOUT it for weeks, and today they're finally going. He's mapped out a route that takes them down a fire road, through an old clear-cut, and over a rocky butte to a steep descent they have to make sitting down, bracing themselves with their heels. The whole thing takes them an hour, but it's the only way to avoid passing close to the owner's house. There are several No Trespassing signs on the main road, and the owner is rumored to have set tripwires along the front of his property line to keep people from crossing his yard. "You think he has guns?" Skye asked before they left, and her father answered, "Probably not as many as Gerry." They've worn the closest to camouflage they can manage without going shopping: her father, olive khakis and a brown jacket; Skye, a dark green raincoat. It isn't raining now, but the ground is wet and slick, and they're covered in mud by the time they reach the riverbank on the opposite side from their house and a mile downstream. They edge along a narrow strip of crumbling earth bordered on one side by a fifteen-foot drop to the water and a solid wall of basalt on the other, until they come to a notch in the rock wide enough for two bodies to pass through side by side.

They've both agreed it's worth the risk of getting caught— though maybe not getting shot—to visit the cave. Her father heard about it from someone in the highway tavern, and he's since done research to confirm: inside are more than a dozen petroglyphs, some at least eight thousand years old. "We're all trespassing," her father said after finally deciding they'd make the trek. "Doesn't matter what the deed says. None of this is our land. And the cave proves it."

It isn't much of a cave, really. She was expecting a long tunnel disappearing into darkness, hanging stalactites, bats in overhead crevices. Instead it's more of a divot in the rock, a scoop carved out by a glacier some ridiculous number of years ago. But the petroglyphs are easy to find, even though her father keeps flickering his flashlight on and off. "This is how it would have looked by fire," he says. "Torches, that's all they would have had to see by, the people who made these."

"Torches wouldn't give me a seizure," she says. "Just leave it on or turn it off."

It's bright enough to see without the extra light. The carvings are clear, deep imprints in the wall above her head: what look like six bear prints above a wavy line. "It was probably a ritual site," her father says. "To pray for good fishing. The line's the river. They wanted to be able to fish as well as bears do. There were still browns here back then."

She tries to imagine what this place would have been like eight thousand years ago, when there were no houses on the river, no roads, just an unbroken blanket of forest with the current cutting through, but mostly she's thinking about the property owner who wants to keep people away from the cave he's claimed as his own, and how irritating people are when they have things they should share but don't. And how she would like to tell her history teacher about seeing this, except then she'll sound like a brownnoser and kids in her class will taunt her, the same ones who spend all day watching other people play video games on YouTube. How frustrating it is to have to act like you don't care about interesting things just because some people are too stupid to know what's interesting and what's not.

Below the carvings and on either side are cruder scratchings in the rock, clearly more recent. Initials, mostly, along with the sort of graffiti she sees in the bathrooms at school: *A + M 4EVR* and *Cam sux cock*. It's all so stupid and irritating that she wishes the property owner would have put an electric fence around the whole cave. Her father seems to be thinking the same thing: "Maybe it's better if no one knows about it," he says.

He had a good plan to get here, but only after they emerge from the cave does it become clear that he has no plan to get them back—or rather that he mistakenly assumed they could return the same way they came. But there's no chance they can scale the steep muddy tracks they left on their way down. He leads them another quarter mile downstream, and they try to climb what looks like an easier grade, but after getting a few hundred yards up the brush closes around them and becomes impenetrable. Another route leads to sheer cliffs. They return to the cave. "No problem," her father says, though his face has frozen into a stiff, toothless half smile she recognizes as the first hint of panic. "We'll just have to cross over to the main road."

"You mean trespass. Across a yard that might be booby trapped."

"I'm sure that's just urban legend. Or rural legend. A myth, in any case."

"And so are the guns?"

"Everyone out here has guns. Except us. If someone comes out, we'll just say we got lost. They're not gonna shoot a kid."

They reach a clearing, at the end of which sits a small cottage with gray shingles and a stone chimney. The driveway, at least, is empty of cars. "We should give this land back," she says. "To the people who made the drawings."

"They're long gone."

"I'm not an idiot. I mean their ancestors."

"Not many of them left either," her father says.

"And not just this spot. All of it."

"History sucks," he says, crouching low behind chest-high salal. "I mean, it's important. You gotta look back. But not much is pretty."

"We should have stayed where we were."

"Then you wouldn't be here."

"Someone else would."

"Someone worse, most likely." He stands up straight, cranes his neck in either direction. "Okay," he says. "On three, we sprint across. I doubt there are any tripwires. But if you hear an alarm, just keep running."

"You're a stellar role model," she says.

"Ready?"

She digs a toe into wet leaves, bends her knees, makes fists at her sides.

"One," he says, and she pushes off, making a straight line for the road, legs pumping hard. She doesn't glance back to see if he's following or if she's left him behind.

15. THE HUNT

THE CABIN SITS A quarter of the way up the canyon at an elevation of just over 1,400 feet. Not high enough to get much snow, and whatever accumulates after a storm usually melts within a day. But once or twice a winter they get a real overnight dumping, two or three inches, and then the landscape is transformed: rocks and ferns become white lumps in the yard, branches sag close to the ground, drifts hang precariously over the riverbank, and falling clumps from tall trees burst on the road in puffy white explosions that linger and sparkle in the still air.

The most exciting moment is when they wake up and look for tracks. It's their chance to glimpse what's hidden to them most of the year, the secrets of their home. Of course they've seen plenty of wildlife in the flesh: mule deer and owls and the blue grouse who thrums for love high up in the canopy every spring. Lewis recently spotted a black bear from a distance on a trail, and Sills once watched a mink slip into the river while he was fishing. And sometimes they'll see tracks in the mud clearly enough to know that the small herd of Roosevelt elk have descended the ridges to drink from a narrow creek that runs through a culvert half a mile east.

But only with the snow do they get the full picture. And how much activity there is right here beside the cabin. Sills follows the three-pronged feet of sparrows down the deck stairs, then the small prints of rodents over the covered dirt path—voles or deer mice—and near the shed she points out what are certainly the wide back feet of a snowshoe hare. Lewis watches her from the deck, drinking his coffee and blowing steam into the crisp air as she creeps close to the ground, her boots and coat pulled on over pajamas. He made this same search when it snowed during the week and has refrained from saying much about it so she can experience it for herself. He lets her scout on her own, calling encouragement when she exclaims over a weasel's tracks near the riverbank. But when she crosses a little hump of raised earth between their property and the neighbor's and calls out, "Whoa!" he slips on his boots to join her.

"Is it a bobcat?" she asks when he comes near. "Or a coyote?"

He bends to examine the prints. The snow is so bright he has to blink a few times to get them clearly in view. The cold rising from the ground penetrates his jeans, though already the air is beginning to warm: the pace of droplets falling from needles has picked up in the last hour, and now they drum a steady beat against the shed roof.

"What is it?" Sills asks with an urgency that makes him want to take his time. Precision, certainty—not usually his strengths. So he adjusts his position, looks at it from a different angle.

There are no claw marks on the toes, and the heel pads have two lobes in front, three in back. Definitely feline. He holds his hand up to it without touching. The track is nearly as wide as his palm and stretches from his wrist to his first knuckle. Far too big for a bobcat. "Holy shit," he says.

"Is it really?" Sills asks with a breathlessness beyond excitement, beyond fear, even—the pure sound of awe.

"I knew they were around," Lewis says. "But not so close."

"It looks like it was heading that way," Sills says, pointing downstream, toward the neighbor's fence.

"But where did it come from?"

She follows the tracks backward. They take her along their section of bank, then up to the far end of the yard, beside which is a stand of Douglas fir that stretches for a hundred yards or so, owned by the neighbor to their east who will eventually, Lewis guesses, clear-cut it for a quick profit. For now, though, it's a dense bit of wilderness from which he can imagine the sleek tawny form of a cougar, with its broad snout and rounded ears and a vertical crease on its forehead, emerging. But instead of heading into the trees, Sills turns toward the house, where she pauses again beneath a window, the small frosted one looking out from their bathroom.

"It stopped right here!" she calls. "Right fucking here!"

It's true: the tracks are joined by the clear imprint of legs, backside, and tail. The enormous creature took a seat next to the house, separated from them by only a foot of wooden siding and insulation and drywall. It might have been sitting here when he came down to piss in the middle of the night, might have caught his scent and felt its mouth watering with the promise of fresh meat.

"I bet it was warming itself," he says. "I kept the stove burning late. Some of our heat must spill out. The snow always melts faster around the foundation."

But Sills isn't listening. She's followed the tracks up through the front yard to the spot where they meet the road. It's clear the cougar came down from the ridge opposite, where the forest ascends another two thousand feet and where the snow will linger into April. There she turns, crawls on hands and knees. She's not wearing gloves, and her hands are bright red, but she doesn't seem bothered by the cold. She creeps alongside the tracks, careful not to cave them in. She stops beneath the bathroom window, sits on her haunches, sniffs the air, licks the back of her hand. Then she's crawling again, down to the bank, across the yard. Clumps of snow stick to her pajamas. A few feet from the garden shed, she goes still. She crouches, holds. Her behind wiggles. She pounces.

"Would have been tasty," she calls. "But I missed. It ran off that way."

"You're still fierce," he says.

"I'm hungry."

"No hare in the fridge, I'm afraid. How about bacon?"

"It'll do," she says and steps carefully over the tracks, which will be long gone by the afternoon.

16. RISK

THE GAME HAS ALREADY been going on for hours, but neither of them wants to call a truce or acknowledge a stalemate. Her father has twenty-five territories, which leaves Skye only seventeen, but she controls the whole of North and South America, has footholds in Asia and Europe, and has been amassing armies to attack from Alaska and Greenland. Her father yawns again, and again glances at the clock, which has moved only a few minutes ahead since the last time he checked. "We really should call it a night," he says. "It's after eleven."

"Just another round," she says.

"You won't want to get up in the morning."

"Two, actually. Then you're toast."

"Neither of us will."

"You can't expect me to quit when you're ahead."

"We should never start this game on a Sunday."

"Not like we've ever finished when we started earlier."

"We can just leave it set up until next weekend."

"You won't have anywhere to eat."

"I'll eat on your bed. You don't mind sleeping on crumbs, right? And a few grease stains?"

"I think it's actually impossible to win. I bet no one in history has actually done it."

"They all die of sleep deprivation first," her father says, but by then it's his turn to place reinforcements and try to attack her vulnerable position in southern Europe from his stronghold in Egypt. She fends him off but, in the process, loses two-thirds of her armies in the territory, which messes up her strategy for the next round. She can continue to build up for her invasion, but if she doesn't protect her flank, she risks a swift retreat. By the time she decides to stick with her original plan, it's nearly midnight. Her father dozes off while she's placing her new armies. He's vulnerable now, hasn't anticipated her sneak attack from Brazil where she piles all her reinforcements. Twelve battalions, plus the four she already had in place. She'll be so tired in first-period algebra tomorrow that she'll have to fight hard to keep her eyes open. Her teacher, Mrs. Daugherty, has a sixth sense for people who aren't prepared or attentive and will spend the whole hour calling on her to catch her out.

But she's not giving up now. She kicks her father's foot to wake him, says, "Get ready to roll," and throws the dice. He blinks as she takes his first two armies, but then he's all the way awake as she gets ready to finish him off. He rolls a two and a three, curses as hers comes up five, four, and one. Victory is swift and sweet, and she does a little dance as she takes her first territory in Africa. "Expel the colonizers!" she shouts, though she knows the entire point of the game is to celebrate colonizing. Any local rebellions her armies will gleefully crush. Global domination is all that matters, and she takes nothing but pleasure in her father's downcast face as he recognizes the scope of her deception.

"Okay, it's on," he says, but rather than regroup and begin placing his reinforcements, he pulls himself up from the floor, twists to pop his back, and heads for the kitchen.

"Where you going?" she calls. "I'm not done kicking your butt yet."

"Making coffee," he says.

"You'll never get to sleep."

"Not letting you blindside me again."

His voice is both angry and secretly delighted, as if he has been waiting a long time for someone to give him a serious challenge. "It's just a game," she calls, though she doesn't believe that for a second. "We can call it a tie."

She's frightened, a little—both that he might agree and that he might not. Coffee beans crack and whir in the electric grinder. Then the sound of water heating up in the Cuisinart, a hiss and burble followed by the steady drip through grounds and filter. The machinery of war coming to life. He's smiling a wicked smile when he returns.

"No one takes Africa from me," he says.

17. JACK

IN LATE JANUARY SILLS comes home from school with the flu, and Lewis agrees with Veronica—over their daughter's objections—that she's too sick to join him for the weekend. So instead he visits her after work on Friday evening. It's the first time he's been in the Salem house since the split, and though he tries to fight it off, nostalgia overwhelms him as he crosses the front porch of the old bungalow he and Veronica bought and restored when Sills was just an infant, resanding and sealing fir floors themselves, hiring an unlicensed electrician—a friend of Veronica's cousin—to replace the knob-and-tube wiring without pulling any permits. He put so much of himself into the place, and now an uncomfortable sense of incompletion gnaws at him, a suspicion that he left a good part of himself behind when he moved out. He doesn't think he'll ever feel whole again.

Sills is clammy when he kisses her forehead, and she can barely open her eyes to look at him, but when she does, her expression is accusatory. "Why couldn't you just let me come?"

she says. "I'd sleep in the car. I don't want to be here all winter."
He finds her wish to be with him gratifying, but when she goes
on, he can't be sure she's longing for the cabin or some location
brewed up by the heat of her fever. "I'll just grab my skis," she
says, though she doesn't own any, has been on them only two
or three times in her life. "We've got to hurry. Jack might be
back any minute." Then her eyes close again. She shivers, rolls
over, lets out a soft snore.

"She decided to read *The Shining*," Veronica explains when
he goes downstairs. "Right before she spiked at a hundred
and three."

To his surprise, she hands him a glass of wine and invites
him to sit. It's something he's hoped to avoid, being a stranger
in his own house, an acquaintance to the woman he loved for
so many years, whose body he once knew as well as his own,
though it's now fading from his memory. He can no longer be
sure whether her birthmark is on her left hip or right. She's
taken up going to a CrossFit gym three times a week and is
slimmer than she was a year ago, though beneath her thick
sweater and fleece pajama bottoms he can't make out her con-
tours. She's become a neutrally attractive figure, with her sandy
hair cut short, her eyes blocked by new progressive lenses in
a teal frame. The sight of her doesn't stir desire in him now,
nor even the sharp pain of their initial separation, just the dull
throb of loss that never quite dissipates. As if to amplify the
ache, Verlaine hops onto his lap, turns two circles, and lies
down across his legs with no acknowledgment that he hasn't
been here for nearly a year. The cat is still skinny after his ill-
ness last fall—salmonella poisoning from an infected bird—and
though he purrs and drools when Lewis scratches his chin, he
otherwise treats this moment as any other in his life, perfectly
ordinary and expected.

"Since I'll miss a weekend with her," Lewis says, to keep them in familiar, businesslike territory, "maybe we can get an extra few days this summer. Right after school ends. Or that week between her theater camp and the trip with your folks."

Again to his surprise, she only shrugs and says, "Sure, that sounds fine," but then gazes at him curiously, as if she's not quite sure what he's doing in the house, or perhaps not sure why he isn't always sitting in the wingback chair they bought together at a vintage store in Portland, long before she was pregnant with Sills, before they decided to give up the commute and move to Salem. He thought of it as a tiny, provincial town when they first settled here; now it's the big, traffic-choked city he escapes every night. "I'm sure she'll be happy to hear that when she's better," Veronica adds, but the curious look remains. Her silence then is an expectant one, but Lewis is determined not to fill it first. He waits, for what he's not certain. Is she going to surprise him with some big announcement? That she's getting remarried, that she's moving across the country and taking Sills with her? He sips the wine, but it's too sweet for him, and he sets the glass on a side table. Then Veronica's expression breaks. She laughs—to herself, it seems—and shakes her head. "I'm being ridiculous."

"About what?"

"Are you really okay out there? By yourself so much of the time?"

"Why wouldn't I be?"

"You're not drinking a lot, are you?"

"What are you talking about?" he asks, though right away he experiences a stab of guilt, along with a flash of his father's angry face when he was about Lewis's age—and Lewis with his hand on a bottle of rye pilfered from his father's liquor cabinet. "I never have more than a beer or two."

She shakes her head again. "I know. I'm being stupid."

"You're the one who puts down a bottle of pinot without thinking twice." He says this sharply, with an edge intended to cut a little. He's paid enough, he thinks, for the things he's done wrong. He doesn't need her to make up things he hasn't done.

But if his words affect her, she doesn't show it. She's laughing again, but it's an uneasy laugh meant to comfort herself, and once more she shakes her head, this time also flicking wrists next to her shoulders as if to wrest them free of something that pinches. "I shouldn't have read it."

"Read what?"

"I just wanted to see what scared her."

"Ronnie, what the hell are you talking about?"

"That stupid book. *The Shining*. She was so freaked out after she finished it, I thought I'd better take a look. It's dumb, I know. And not even that well written. But it put images in my head."

Now it's Lewis's turn to laugh, and his is a bitter, self-righteous laughter, disruptive enough to make Verlaine momentarily lift his head. "You think I'll go nuts."

"Of course not."

"And what, come after you with an axe? Stick my evil face through a hole in the door? Here's Lewis?"

"In the book it's a mallet."

"Jesus, Veronica. I'm still me."

"I know."

"I don't get drunk. I make it to work every day. Usually on time. I'm keeping up with the bills. I feed the kid healthy food. We have a pretty good time together, mostly. What else do you want from me?"

"I'm sorry," she says.

"I'm not even that depressed anymore," he says, though now he knows he may be pushing his advantage too far. Better to keep her on the defensive and not relinquish the upper hand with claims he can't fully defend. "Not all the time, at least."

"I just get worried," she says.

"That I'll lose my shit?"

"That I'll stop knowing who you are." Her strange look has disappeared, the uneasy smile replaced by the reddened upper lip that means she's holding back tears. "That's my own choice," she goes on. "And I don't regret it. It's just strange."

"You know who I am. I haven't changed. I'm not gonna snap."

"You have changed," she says.

"How so?"

"You're better out there. Better without me. A better dad."

"Shit, Ronnie. Are you trying to make me cry?"

He's stopped petting the cat, and Verlaine reaches out a paw and presses it to his belly, a reminder to continue. If he doesn't start stroking soon, claws will poke through his shirt. Can it be true that he's changed so much if the cat still treats him the same as ever?

"I'm the one who's going nuts, obviously," Veronica says.

And then from upstairs comes Sills's voice, frightened and weary, calling out, "Where are my skis? Where'd you put my fucking skis?"

"No more scary books," he says. "For either of you."

18. HYPHENATED

FOR CHRISTMAS, HER GRANDPA Norgrove—her mother's father—gave her a box of family documents. Beneath the stack of old papers was a hundred-dollar bill, which her mother says makes the gift even more obnoxious. Her grandfather always hands her ancient, musty items passed down from his own parents and grandparents or purchased decades ago in curiosity shops: hand-painted Russian icons, carved wooden boxes, tintype photographs in rotting cardboard frames, a letter signed by John Glenn when he was senator of Ohio. What does she want with any of it? The hundred dollars, her mother says, is a bribe to keep her from objecting when he gives her his garbage to make room in his office closet.

But now, despite her mother's gripes, she's gotten interested in the papers, which her great-grandmother kept and organized to record the family's history. Skye talked her mother into getting her a DNA test and signing on to a website where they can find other relatives, and she's since been working on an extended family tree. Her grandfather and the other Norgroves—all except her mother—are unreasonably proud of their legacy. They can trace their line back to French Huguenots, one of whom fought with Washington's army at Princeton and earned a military pension and bounty land in Kentucky, where the family lived for several generations before selling their farm and moving north to open a foundry on the shore of Lake Erie. Her great-grandmother stayed active in the Daughters of the American Revolution well into her seventies, and in the trove of documents are several letters in which she requested—then demanded—that her ancestor be recognized with a monument.

Skye has other homework to do, but she's hoping to convince her history teacher to let her use this material for an upcoming research paper instead of just checking books out of the library—or listening to the *Hamilton* soundtrack as June plans to—so she tells herself it's perfectly reasonable to spend all weekend jotting down notes and filling out branches on the tree, especially since it's dark and raining and her father is happy enough lying on the couch reading magazines. At one point, however, he raises his head and says, "You know, you might not like everything you find in there."

"I already saw there's a relative who fought on the British side, if that's what you mean."

"It's not," he says.

He doesn't add any more, and she doesn't ask, not until half an hour later when she finds a copy of a bill of sale. It takes her a few minutes to decipher the script, and when she does, she mutters, "You gotta be kidding."

"Sorry," he says.

"You knew?"

"Your mom always suspected. But she never wanted to

go anywhere near those papers. Your grandpa tried to unload them on her a few times. Whenever he found a suspicious mole and thought his time was up. She always gave them back."

She wishes she'd also planned to just listen to the musical, though her teacher already spent a whole class period telling them what was inaccurate about its portrayal of Hamilton, which made him out to be an abolitionist, though he, too, bought and sold slaves. She counts the items on the bill, which also includes several horses and a buggy. "Fourteen," she says. "They sold fourteen people in 1822."

"That's when the cotton gin really took off," he says. "Big demand in the Deep South."

"This is the worst thing I've ever seen," she says, but she isn't quite sure if that's how she really feels about it or just how she thinks she's supposed to feel. It's a strange experience, to find herself connected to something horrible, which somehow makes her feel less connected to herself, as if she's reading her own name in a dreary textbook.

"People try to make up for it," he says. "Reparations."

She waves the hundred-dollar bill she was planning to spend on a pair of roller skates. "I'm not taking any more of his blood money."

"His family lost everything in the Depression. Then made it back by investing in coal. So a different kind of blood money than the original."

"I don't want it," she says and tries to throw the bill away from her, but it just flips in the air and lands back on the table.

"That's before your grandpa dropped enough acid to melt a horse's brain and joined a new age cult. His parents cut him off after that. So this money doesn't come from them either. It's all his own blood money. From trading pharmaceutical stocks, mostly."

"I'll burn it," she says.

"You could donate it to the NAACP. Or the Black Panthers."

"Can we do your side of the tree?"

He lays his magazine face down on the coffee table and pulls himself, with difficulty, off the couch. "What do you have so far?"

She shows him: one notch up from herself, with the hyphenated last name she's always hated, she's written down his name and his sister's—her aunt Linda—and before that his parents and her bubby's siblings, but she can't remember her papa's brother's name. He helps her with that, and then adds his grandparents, their numerous brothers and sisters, a handful of cousins, none of whom she's ever met. When it comes to his great-grandparents, he knows the name of only one, his paternal great-grandfather—knows, too, that he had a brother, but not his name.

"That's it?" she says. "Mom's goes back like twelve generations."

"These are all the ones who immigrated," he says. "The rest stayed in Europe."

"What happened to them?"

"Do you really want to know?"

She says she does, though she isn't sure it's true.

"Hang on," he says and climbs the stairs to the loft. She hears him rummaging in the desk she never sees him use, though occasionally when she goes up there, she finds unopened bills sitting on its otherwise empty surface, his checkbook nowhere in sight. She expects him to come down with a musty box similar to the one her grandfather gave her, only smaller, or at least a file folder thick with papers. But he descends slowly, unfolding a single sheet on the way. As he glances it over, an unfamiliar look settles on his face, one that suggests he can't believe what he's just seen, even though he's obviously seen it before.

"I printed this out a few years ago. From the Yad Vashem database. I don't know how many are actually related to us, but that's the town my great-grandfather came from."

She reads down the list. Sixteen entries, all with the last name Nelson. The place of residence, too, is the same for each: Sochaczew, Poland. There's a column marked *birth year*, and here there's a variety of numbers: 1912, 1870, 1936, 1940. The last column is labeled *fate*. And in each box below, one word: *murdered*.

She doesn't say anything. This document seems no more real, no more a part of her story than the bill of sale, though maybe easier to imagine describing to her history teacher. The family tree is lopsided and hideous, one branch cut off close to the trunk, the other sprawling and weighted with ugly deeds. If it were a real tree, the first storm to pass would topple it and crush everything underneath. She wishes she had nothing to do with it, that it had nothing to do with her, but there's her stupid hyphenated name near the base, as if she were the source of the whole thing, its original seed.

The hundred-dollar bill lies face down in front of her. On its back is the engraving of an old building with a clock tower; in the foreground a statue stands between a pair of staked saplings. She has no idea what building it is or why it's important enough to be on money. It's never occurred to her to wonder until now.

19. REWARD

"Look at that," he says, tapping the dashboard clock. "We're five minutes early."

"Someone should give you a prize," Sills says.

Before he can respond, she's out of the car, running through the huge middle school parking lot to catch up with kids piling out of yellow buses—maybe to make it look as if she were on one of them, as she is every other day of the week. Only then does he realize she's wearing nothing but a thin cotton sweater over leggings, though it can't be more than forty-five degrees outside and misting, her bony ankles bare above her sneakers. Still, as he watches her disappear into the ugly brick building with a low-slung overhanging roof like the bill of a cap shading sensitive eyes, he does feel a sense of accomplishment. It doesn't take much these days—remembering to pick up a package at the post office will buoy him for a week or more.

Despite his daughter's sarcasm, he does want to reward himself. Why not, if no one else will? So on his way to work he stops at a donut shop. It was once a Dunkin' Donuts, but the new owners, a Syrian couple with two teenage boys, didn't want to pay the franchise fee, so they changed the name to Drink 'n' Donuts and added an espresso machine they struggle to operate. Lewis hasn't been here in months, but the proprietor greets him as if he stopped in just days ago. "Welcome back, my friend!" he shouts as he carries a stack of empty trays into the back room. His wife, at the counter, gives her typical bored look and waits with a finger poised above the cash register.

It's the only shop in town that reminds him of places he frequented as a boy in New Jersey, the mixture of aggressive friendliness and indifference, the pressure of a mild hustle. He knows before he orders that the transaction won't be a straightforward one. He pretends to scan the racks of donuts behind the counter for a good thirty seconds, though he knew what he wanted when he first walked in: one cinnamon, one chocolate glazed, and a cup of black coffee. He hopes the appearance of deliberation might forestall the negotiating he knows he can't avoid. But when he names his items, the woman's finger continues to hover above the buttons. "Only two?" she asks.

He pats his belly, which is still mostly flat, though some days it strains against his belt more than he would like. "Got to watch myself."

"What about your family? Don't they get any?"

"I won't see my daughter until the weekend," he says, and when he detects no sign of sympathy in her face, adds, "They'd be stale by then."

From the back, her husband shouts, "Never stale! Always fresh!"

"Your employees, then," she says. "You bring them donuts, you're the best boss in the world."

He doesn't tell her he's one of only three people in his entire unit, which covers media relations and internal communication for the DOT. His supervisor does all the talking to reporters, and a coworker handles social media posts. Both of them are overweight. No one reports to him.

"They don't work hard enough to deserve a reward," he says and performs a villainous laugh, to which the woman feigns outrage—not over his treatment of imaginary underlings but his neglect of her beautiful product. She abandons the register and approaches the racks, pointing out full bins of donuts no one buys: heavily frosted, maple-flavored, cream-filled. He wants nothing to do with any of them.

"Everyone needs more than two," she says, already pulling out a box that fits a dozen. "How about these nice hearts. Special for Valentine's."

Valentine's Day has already passed—he spent it tipsy in a tavern whose door handle is meant to look like an axe plunged into wood—but he knows better than to question their freshness. "My office is small," he says firmly, making certain his voice leaves no room for doubt or hedging. "Half a dozen. Two chocolate glazed, two cinnamon, two old-fashioned."

Before she can argue, the door opens behind him with an electronic jingle that seems unnecessary since the place is narrow and cramped. There's hardly room for three people to stand at the counter because of the enormous soft-drink refrigerator to its left and three small tables to its right. Plus, he's never seen the woman standing anyplace where she could fail to see whoever walks in the door. Now it's a trio of teenagers, two boys in skate shoes and hooded black sweatshirts, a girl in shredded camo pants and lots of safety pins on a denim jacket. He approves of their fashion, which isn't so different from his fashion at their age, though he'd never been adept enough at skateboarding to wear Vans without feeling self-conscious. The girl is the toughest looking of the bunch, with black eyelids and tiny pink pigtails sticking up like a baby goat's horns. They call out their orders without waiting for the woman to ask for them.

"You should be in school!" her husband shouts from the back. "Get out of here!"

"We're seniors now," one of the boys calls to him, wearily, as if he's said this many times before. "We don't start till second period."

Lewis wonders if he'd appreciate the girl's style as much if it were his daughter's, but he can't quite imagine Sills with such a jaded expression, her countenance full of fight, expecting people to get in her way and knowing she had no choice but to push past them. To his surprise, the woman sets his box aside and fills the kids' orders first, packing an extra donut—the heart-shaped ones—into each of their bags. They slap their change onto the counter and bounce to the door. She calls after them, "If you see Samir, tell him his mother needs his help after school."

The door lets loose its cheerful electronic ring, and the girl calls over her shoulder, "I'll tell him, but you know Sammy don't listen to nobody. Not even me." The kids' swagger wavers when the wind hits them, and the rain, and then they're running across the parking lot with their donut bags hugged to chests. Maybe he wishes such toughness on Sills, but not the need for it, given how that need usually arises.

When he turns back to the counter, the woman's look has softened—for the first time, he thinks, since he's been frequenting the shop. "They're good to our boys," she says. "Not like most of the kids at that stupid school. Or their stupid teachers." Her face tightens again, and she shoves his box of donuts across the counter. She's done haggling, it seems. She's also forgotten his coffee, but he supposes he's had enough already. He pays, thanks her, calls goodbye to her husband, who shouts after him, "My friend! Come see us more often!"

When he arrives at the office—ten minutes late—his supervisor exclaims over the donuts and forgets to ask him about the news release he should have finished yesterday. "What's the special occasion?" his coworker asks, a little skeptically, as if she doubts his motives. She's been working for the state for nearly thirty years and is unnerved by the slightest change in routine; it's taken her months to adjust to a new meeting schedule, about which she continues to complain every week.

"Just felt like we all needed a little reward," he says. "For all our hard work."

His supervisor takes a chocolate glazed, his favorite. So does his coworker. Lewis is left with cinnamon, a good second choice, though it's dry, a little stale, and sticks in his throat without coffee to wash it down.

20. THE PATH

HER FATHER LIKES TO start projects but has a hard time finishing them. At the Salem house, he cleared a spot to grow boysenberries, killed the grass along the fence by covering it with newspaper and mulch, sank posts in concrete, and even strung one wire between them. But he never managed to drive to the nursery to buy the starts, and the posts sat empty for two seasons before her mother finally planted grape cuttings from a neighbor's yard. Those have since rooted and begun to send up tendrils where boysenberry canes were meant to grow. "Just as tasty, and no thorns," her mother said, though Skye agrees with her father—nothing beats boysenberries, if you actually have them.

The same pattern often repeats itself in the cabin. In the fall he decided to paint the loft, but he only got as far as priming two walls, and since then cans of paint have sat unopened beneath his bed. When she asks about it, he says, "Fumes were too strong. Need to wait till I can keep the windows open."

His most recent project is a stone path, meant to meander from the deck to the riverbank. On an unexpectedly dry, mostly sunny Saturday in February, they drive up into the hills and gather flat pieces of basalt—or reasonably flat, with the idea that later he can chip away any lumpy bits that stick out with a rock hammer when he's laying them in place.

"Do we have a rock hammer?" she asks.

"Not yet. But I'm sure they're easy enough to buy."

To her surprise, he actually looked up the rules about taking rocks from National Forest land, how much is allowed without a permit, though of course he has no scale and can only guess at the weight. Skye enjoys the process, in any case, because under every slab she turns over are new surprises. Scurrying potato bugs and centipedes, curled-up slugs, a little black salamander that darts away before she can snag it. Some of the spiders make her jump, especially the ones with huge smooth abdomens that look as if they're about to burst open with hundreds of babies, but as long as she has gloves on, even those don't keep her from turning over the next rock. In one spot they hear the warning call of pikas—that distinctive *meep* like the cartoon roadrunner's—coming from an old rockslide, and she thinks she spots one ducking into a gap between two large slabs, a flash of fur in her periphery, though by the time she turns to face it directly, all is still.

They fill up the back of her father's car until its rear bumper is at least half a foot lower than the front. "You sure that's under the limit?" she asks, though she doesn't actually care. Her arms are sore from carrying rocks, but she's eager to get them home and start arranging them in the yard.

He gestures to the hillside covered in black and gray shards. "I think we've left enough."

When they get back to the cabin, she starts to pull rocks from the car and place them in front of the deck's lowest step, but he stops her before she's laid more than three. "We've got to dig them in," he says. "Make sure they're good and stable."

"Let's do it then," she says and has a vision of the path winding among the ferns, moss growing between the stones by the time she returns next week.

But her father takes his time unloading the rocks from the trunk, making stacks along the side of the shed, at first haphazardly, then rearranged by size. "It'll make things easier when we're laying them out," he says, and she starts digging a spot for the first one.

Before he finishes unloading, he goes inside to use the bathroom. She keeps digging. Half an hour passes. She's placed the first three stones but can't get them to sit flat without wobbling when she stands on them. "Dad!" she calls, but he doesn't answer. Inside, she finds him on the couch, reading one of the fishing magazines that has occupied much of his time since trout season ended. "Aren't we gonna finish?"

"My back needs a break," he says. "I'll be ready in a few minutes."

She returns to the yard, fiddles with the rocks she's already placed, then decides it might be more efficient to break up the soil first. So she grabs the pickaxe from the shed, swings it a few times, quickly runs out of breath. When she catches it, she calls, "Dad! Are you coming?"

But when she goes inside again, he's in the kitchen, flipping a pair of grilled cheese sandwiches on an electric griddle. "A little sustenance first, right?" he says. It's true, she's hungry, but she wants to get the path going while they have the momentum. "We've got plenty of light left," he says.

But after they eat, he tells her he needs a few minutes to digest, and then he falls asleep on an armchair, chin on chest. She digs in a few more rocks and then wakes him. "Okay, okay," he says. "I'm on my way. Just let me get a glass of water first."

He agrees with her that maybe their best bet is to dig out the full shape of the path before laying too many stones, so he spends an hour working the pick, stretching after every few swings, churning up the earth in a wide swath for about a dozen yards before deciding the path needs a curve earlier, and backing up to start again. By the time the sun hits the top of the trees to the west, they've got a huge, chopped-up square of dirt with ten stones of varying flatness lying at strange angles to each other, nothing looking quite like the perfectly arranged puzzle she imagined. Only two of the rocks stay still when she walks across them.

"We've got all day tomorrow," her father says and goes inside to start dinner. But she stays out until it's all the way dark, turning the rocks one way and then another, trying to get at least a couple to fit snugly against each other, or at least to fit in a way that isn't unsightly.

Tomorrow, she thinks, shaking out her aching arms, wiggling her cramped fingers. But in the morning it's raining again, and her father says there's no point in going back to work until it lets up a bit; all they'll do is turn the ground to mud. But the ground is turning to mud already. She watches from the window as water fills up the square they've dug, making it look even more like an ugly wound they've gouged into their once-beautiful yard. The piles of stone beside the shed seem precarious, ready to topple at any moment. The rain doesn't quit all morning, all afternoon, and eventually she gives up any hope she has—not just for finishing the path this weekend but finishing it ever. She knows the best she can hope for is that the hole will fill with leaves and fir needles, that moss will eventually grow over the collapsed pile of rocks beside the shed and make them look like they belong there. Her father, she knows, has already forgotten the path; his imagination has moved on to new projects he'll start and never finish, and until she's old enough or strong enough to finish them on her own, she'll have to live with his wreckage.

When he drives her to school on Monday morning, she listens to the rattle of rocks in the back of the car, the ones he hasn't yet unloaded, the ones that will stay until he needs the space for something else.

21. HEAT

WHEN SILLS WAS AN infant and toddler, Lewis often found himself distracted—by exhaustion, by nostalgia for a time without responsibility, by his dreamy nature—at moments when he should have been paying close attention. Once she choked on a cracker shaped like a rabbit, and he had to stick his finger in her throat to get it out. Another time she grabbed Verlaine's flank with both hands, and the cat bit holes in her cheek. Later he pinched the same cheek in the clip of a bicycle helmet when he was getting her ready for a ride.

But the moment that haunts him most came during her first winter, a frigid January night when Veronica was out at a meeting. He bounced her and played her music—J. J. Cale's first album always made her sleepy—and set her down in her crib with the stuffed sloth she loved and the blanket with satin edges she later carried around everywhere. By the time Veronica returned, he was bundled on the couch in blankets of his own, watching a movie, proud of himself for getting the kid to bed by himself. But when she went into Sills's room, she let out a cry. He's never gotten over the feeling that sound triggered, a cold dread that made him want to run—not to Sills's room, which is where his feet led him, but out the front door, down the street, away from town, as far as he could get. *I killed her child*, he thought, though he could see that Sills was alive, just shivering, her face pale, lips nearly purple. "She must have kicked her blanket off," he said as Veronica warmed her against her chest. "She never called out or anything." Only after color came back to her cheeks did Sills let out a ferocious howl, and Veronica's eyes settled on him, not with accusation as he expected, or anger, or even disappointment, just pity—a look that anticipated all that would follow between them.

And that's why he's particularly horrified when the power shuts off in the middle of a freezing February afternoon, the lights blinking out, the baseboard heaters ticking as they cool. He knows he's late paying the bills, not because he doesn't have the money, only because he can't ever remember to buy stamps and drop them in a mailbox on his way to work. He decided, when he first bought the cabin, not to have mail delivered here but to a post office box in Millburg—thinking he wouldn't be here during the week to pick it up—and he hasn't gotten around to making the change. Now he must have passed three late notices and several warnings. He calls a number on the latest bill, sits on hold for forty-five minutes as Sills shivers in her coat and hat in front of the woodstove he's been struggling to light because he let the firewood get wet. There's a lot of smoke whenever he opens the door but no flames. He can't find any newspaper—he reads the *Times* online at work and doesn't bother with local news—so instead tears up pieces of mail, including other bills he needs to pay, and touches the ends of more lit matches to them. They flare up, curl, smolder. The kindling doesn't catch.

"You know you can set up automatic payments," Sills says. "That's what Mom does."

"I'll do that as soon as someone picks up the goddamn phone," he says. But when someone does, she tells him he'll have to call customer service on Monday to pay the bill. If there are no lines down, there's nothing she can do for him now. He stuffs more mail into the stove, and a tiny flame dances along the slanted line of a twig.

"Ah, now we won't freeze to death," Sills says, and there's that bluish tint to her lips, along with the impulse to move his feet, lift his knees, run as far away as his legs will carry him.

"Hang on a sec," he says and rummages in a closet until he finds a few chemical hand warmer packs, along with an extra pair of gloves. He pulls blankets from both their beds and piles them around her until only her head sticks out.

"I'm supposed to stay like this till Monday?"

"I guess I better take you home."

"This is home."

"When your mom finds out—"

"Wait a minute," she says. "Check my backpack."

"What should I be looking for?"

"My geography notebook."

"And that's going to help how?"

"Just bring it."

He does, and before he can stop her, she opens it and tears half the pages off the spiral binding. She rips them into strips and hands them over. "Don't you need these?" he asks. "Won't there be a test?"

"Nothing but doodles," she says. "Teacher's a moron. Thinks we don't know how to read a map."

"Most people don't."

"Not getting hypothermia is more important than knowing the capital of South Dakota."

"Fargo?"

"Who knows," she says as he twists the paper into sticks. She tears more pages off the metal coil, and he crumples them into balls. All of it goes in, along with more damp kindling, and this time the flames are quick and hot, and the wood catches enough to try a small log on top, and this, too, begins to burn at one end. Soon the stove is kicking off enough heat for Sills to throw off one of the blankets.

Only then does Lewis realize how cold he's gotten. His teeth begin to chatter, and to hide it, he goes to look for candles. There are none in the kitchen drawer where he expects to find them and none in the closet where he keeps his camping gear. The only flashlight has no batteries. He pulls out sleeping bags instead and rolls them out in front of the fire.

"We'll be fine if we sleep in here," he says. "But it'll be too dark soon to do much."

"I guess you just need to tell me lots of stories," she says.

"At least we don't need to worry about the food going bad. Colder in here than inside the fridge."

"Like you used to when I was little."

"No hot meals, though. Sandwiches, I suppose."

Sills has pulled off her hat. Static makes her hair cling to one cheek and stick up in the back. A hint of pink has returned to her face. "You better come up with good ones," she says. "Otherwise you'll spend the next two days hearing me complain about how I'm losing my mind."

"We can roast marshmallows in the stove. And maybe warm some water for hot chocolate on top."

"I like those ones you used to tell. You know, about how things came to be called this or that or whatever?"

"Origin stories?"

"How come you never tell them anymore?"

"I'll get some more wood. Then I will."

"Start it first," she says and stretches out on the pile of blankets, hands behind her head. "So I don't die of boredom."

"Did I ever tell you the one about where marshmallows come from?"

"A marsh," she says. "Obviously."

"That's what they want you to think," he says. "But there's a lot more to it."

"Tell me," she says.

22. THE BEST

ONE SATURDAY HER FATHER takes her to Portland. To get a city fix, he says, and break up the long, monotonous winter. They'll go to Powell's, grab some dinner, catch a show. He's even booked them at a hotel for the night so they can have a fancy breakfast in the morning. Of course she's excited—how could she not be?—though all week she's been imagining the dark, solitary days in the cabin, listening to rain pinging the roof, thinking melancholy thoughts. If anyone asked, she would have said she was dreading those days, though now that she won't have them, she worries she'll lack some crucial element of the weekend and wonders how she'll be ready for the week to follow.

Her parents used to take her into the city regularly when she was younger, but more than a year has passed since she's been here, and everything looks bigger than she remembered. The glass towers along the south waterfront, the freeway bridge soaring over the Willamette, the river itself three times as wide here as when it passes through Salem, and the bookstore that takes up an entire block. She picks out a couple of novels with creepy covers—she's into vampires lately—but the number of choices overwhelms her, and even when her father, who has a dozen paperbacks in his basket, encourages her to pick out more, she deflects and says two is plenty.

"You'll finish them by the end of the week," he says, "and then you'll tell everyone you're bored to death."

She smiles a smile that feels pained and false but can't explain any further. "I'm good," she says.

"Best bookstore in the world," he says. "You sure you don't need more time to look around?"

"I'm sure."

On their way across town, he points out places he lived before meeting her mom: a condo in the Pearl District, a brick apartment building downtown, the attic of a dilapidated Victorian across the river, the basement of another twenty blocks east.

"You lived everywhere," she says.

"I was here twelve years. Feels like a lifetime. Literally, in your case."

"Why'd you move around so much?" she asks.

He shifts in his seat—a little uncomfortable, it seems— and says, "The attic was my favorite, but the landlord raised the rent, and I couldn't afford it anymore. Other places . . . I lived with different . . . people. Sometimes they got sick of me, sometimes I—"

"Girlfriends," she says.

"A few."

They stop for pizza on a little side street, at a place marked only by a tiny wooden sign. She wouldn't have realized it was a restaurant if she passed it on her own, but the second he opens the door the smell of oregano and garlic floods her nose. Her father greets the woman behind the counter by name, and she gives him a huge, open-mouthed smile. A young woman in her early twenties, Skye guesses, wearing a crop top that shows off a flat stomach and pierced belly button. Too young to have been one of the girlfriends he lived with before she was born. She would have been Skye's age then, or younger. He introduces her, but Skye doesn't catch her name. "Oh my God!" the young woman squeals. "This is Silly? She's gotten so huge! I haven't seen you since you were, like, a tiny toddler munching on breadsticks."

"I've been here before?" Skye asks.

The owner, it turns out, is an old friend of her father's, and this is his daughter. The former carries their pizza out when it's ready, sits at the table with them, and talks to her father about people she's never heard of. He's her father's age, maybe a little older, with just as much gray in his hair, but he's broader and thicker around the middle, and his arms are covered in faded tattoos. "Gene makes the best pie on the West Coast," her father says. "Would be the best in the world, but, you know, nothing beats New Jersey pizza."

"Always with Jersey," Gene says and gives Skye a wink that scrunches up half his face. "You haven't lived there in, what, thirty years?"

"Almost."

Skye agrees that it's good, maybe the best pizza she's ever had, but when her father presses her, she can't say any more than "I like it a lot." He gives her a long, scrutinizing look, and she knows she's being shy and weird, but she can't help it. She doesn't understand why, except that she's having a hard time thinking of her father living anywhere but in the cabin by the river. She can hardly even picture him in the Salem house anymore, though he's been gone not even a full year. How could he have lived whole lives before she was even born? She tries to imagine herself living here, eating the best pizza, browsing in the best bookstore, sharing an attic with someone who might eventually get sick of her, and all of it makes her clam up and give everyone the odd smile that hurts her face.

She's relieved when they make their way downtown for the show, relishing the twenty minutes before it starts, when she can sit quietly reading the program in the huge, buzzing concert hall, and even more, the moment when the lights go dim. It's a musical production of *The Lion King*, something she's wanted to see for a long time. Her father hates musicals, she knows, though he's never admitted it to her. He's suffered through summer productions her theater camp has put on for the past several years—she's had small roles and worked on the tech crew, though this summer she's planning to audition for a lead part—and after those she recognizes a similarly stiff smile on his face as the one she's been wearing all day. She appreciates his finding something she would like, and she knows the tickets are expensive, but they're so far away from the stage she can hardly see the actors' faces, and the music sounds too slick as it blasts through the huge bank of speakers—as if it were a recording, though she can see the live orchestra. During intermission, he buys her a chocolate bar, and she thanks him, and then thanks him again after the show is over, but everything she says feels forced and overly formal, as if someone else is saying it.

The sky should be dark when they leave the auditorium, but there are so many lights everywhere that it's a hazy orange

instead. Inside the hotel, too, is overly bright, a huge chande-
lier overhead—not the old-fashioned kind with lots of crystals
but one made of polished chrome with a square of frosted glass
covering each bulb. Everything in the place looks futuristic, or
someone's idea of the future twenty years ago; the furniture in
their room is boxy, with hard edges, including the frames of
the two queen-sized beds. The mattress, however, droops like a
sinkhole when she lies on it, nearly swallowing her. "I like it,"
she says, when her father asks what she thinks. "It's cool." But
again, she can't find any more words. They take turns washing
up and brushing their teeth in the bathroom with square light
fixtures and chrome faucets and then lie on their beds in the
dark. Through the window comes the sound of cars passing on
the street below, people talking on the sidewalk, music from a
nearby bar. Her father's breath is even but not the ragged, sputtering version that suggests he's asleep.

"Can we go home?" she asks.

"Now?"

"I'm sorry," she says.

"No, it's fine."

"I had a great time," she says. "I just—"

"I get it," he says. "Let's go."

"Are you sure?"

"There's zero chance I'll be able to sleep on this thing."

"I like it here," she says. "But . . . I don't know."

"I'm with you," he says. "Hundred percent."

They pack up and sneak past the registration desk as if
they're skipping out without paying, though of course a clerk
already ran her father's credit card. They're giggling when they
reach the parking garage, and then as they speed down the freeway, with all its bright lights flashing through the windshield,

they talk about how dull *The Lion King* was, how sentimental, how melodramatically the actors played their parts.

"Gene's pizza's gone downhill since the last time I was there," her father says. "It's still pretty good, but it definitely used to be better."

"I like Powell's," she says. "But, I mean, it's so big, and you can't really concentrate, or sit down and read a few pages—"

"Small bookstores are great. Much cozier."

By the time they reach the winding road along the river, they're belting out songs from the musical in funny voices, her father doing a Russian accent—the only one he's good at—Skye trying out what her theater camp director has called a Scarlett O'Hara, though her father says she sounds less like a Southern belle than an old coot from the mountains, a gold prospector defending his claim. They laugh and argue, and she watches small green signs tick by, marking the miles until they're home. Outside, it's finally pitch black, nothing visible beyond the beams their headlights throw in front of them.

23. THE CODE

HE'S TRIED CHAMOMILE, WHICH did nothing, and kava, which gave him strange dreams. Tonight he takes a valerian capsule, which makes him belch bitter, herby clouds as he stares at the sloped ceiling, listening to rain battering the roof and wind rattling the gutters. After a while he begins picturing tree limbs crashing through the shingles or spearing him through the window, and he goes downstairs, where a few coals are still glowing in the woodstove. He listens at Sills's door, hears nothing, and as he did when she was an infant, slips in to make sure she's breathing. He never anticipates disaster in the middle of the day. Why is it so much easier to imagine calamity after the clock passes midnight?

Her chest rises and falls beneath her blanket. Her hair drapes across a cheek. She looks younger asleep, a child who might cry out in the night and need his comfort, though it was usually her mother who comforted her when she called, while he put a pillow over his head and returned to dreams. The rain sounds louder down here, each drop a small bucketful, and now he worries that the river will overflow its banks and sweep them away while they sleep, which wakes him even more. The valerian burps won't subside, in any case, so he stretches out on the living room couch and tries to read a book—a history of the Silk Road—but can't concentrate enough to get through a paragraph. He tries a mystery instead but finds he doesn't much care about the dead body discovered beneath a staircase, nor how it got there. So he pulls out the fly-tying guide he's been studying for the past year without yet having successfully tied his own fly. His fingers are too thick, he decides, or else he drinks too much coffee to keep them still. Too much coffee to sleep, also, and now it's after two, and he's quite sure he'll be awake at dawn, though at this time of year dawn isn't easy to distinguish, the clouds so dense they hardly brighten when the sun breaches the horizon.

It's dark enough now that he can't see much when he cups his hands around his eyes and presses his face to the window. A distant light from a neighbor's house reflects on water in the backyard, closer than he expects, and he thinks the river is indeed flooding, that soon the cabin will be floating down the canyon. But then he makes out a lumpy edge around the reflection, spiky fern fronds beyond it. Just a puddle. The river is nowhere near topping its bank. And if it did, it would flood the opposite side first, where the bank is a few feet lower, the ground sloping for a few hundred yards before reaching an upsurge of ridge that forms the canyon's southern wall.

The fly-tying guide does nothing for him now—it'll be a month before he can stand in the water again, attempting to cast—so instead he picks up Sills's phone, which rests face down on the coffee table. There's no signal, as usual, but he opens it anyway. Veronica told him the passcode, said they should monitor her use from time to time. At her age, it's important to know what she's looking at online, who she's communicating with on social media. There have been too many reports of young girls and adolescents preyed upon and victimized—both he and Veronica heard the same harrowing report on the radio about Portland teenagers coerced into prostitution—to allow her the privacy she has often demanded. "If you want a phone at twelve, these are the conditions," her mother told her.

Up to now, Lewis hasn't done any of the monitoring, and he feels instantly guilty when he enters the last number and Sills's background appears, a close-up of Verlaine with his tongue sticking out. Without internet, he can't look at her browser history, but he can open her text messages and see who she's been chatting with. Before doing so, he listens carefully again, waiting for her to step out and catch him in the act. *Your mother told me to*, he already imagines himself saying when she accuses him of betrayal, ready to betray Veronica without hesitation.

But all is still quiet behind her door, her breath even as the rain eases to a steady patter. The most recent messages are from someone named "Gzl" in her contacts, and they are nothing but a series of emojis: half a dozen hearts, a smiley face winking. Sills replied with a GIF of a donkey kicking up its back legs. There must be communication of some sort in this exchange, but not one Lewis can understand. It's a secret code, like those the Germans used during World War II, but even more impenetrable because of its inanity.

Most of the threads are similar. None of the names as she's recorded them are identifiable as friends he's heard about, though he suspects "J.Low" is the notorious June, who has been a demanding and fickle friend, making Sills cry on multiple occasions, though after ignoring her for a week or two, she always comes back around, telling Sills she's her most important friend—she never says *best*—and that she'll never make it through middle school without her. In their most recent exchange, "J.Low" has said, *idk, you rite lst tm*, to which Sills replied, *thx, beetch*. He takes this to mean they are currently on good terms, about which he feels ambivalent—he doesn't want Sills to suffer, but he also wishes June would just fuck off for good and stop messing with his girl.

The only contact names fully legible to him are "Bubs" and "mom." The first is Lewis's own mother, who likes to send Sills inspirational platitudes, the most recent of which reads, *If you want the rainbow, you gotta put up with the rain.* Sills always answers her dutifully: *Love you!* or *Miss you!* or *I wish I had more of your choc crinkle cookies. Will you send some?*

He feels especially guilty opening the messages from Veronica, but then thinks, with a bitterness as foul as his valerian breath, *You told me to.* Most of the exchanges are practical—when she's coming to pick Sills up, where Sills should meet her, what she's planning to make for dinner. But there are some Lewis finds as mysterious as those between Sills and her friends. *You sure?* her mother asked a couple of weeks ago—unprompted, it seems, and without context—and Sills responded, *Jst gettn wet.* He has no idea what this means and isn't sure he wants to know. If he were to break the code, what would he hope to discover? That they're talking about him? Or that they never mention him at all? Which would be worse?

In only one exchange is his presence definitive: on what must have been a Monday morning, about three weeks ago, Veronica wrote, *Did you eat enough this weekend? Need me to bring some snacks after school?* to which Sills answered, *Dd made grn beans. Real gd.* He remembers those green beans, which he managed to avoid overcooking. Sills ate two portions, though she hardly picked at the fish tacos he'd made them to accompany. Should he take this as a sign of her support, defending him against her mother's subtle suggestion that he's not capable of feeding her properly, of doing his parental duty? Veronica wrote back an hour later: *I'll bring you an energy bar when I pick you up.* And then Sills, with more mystery than ever: *Tuff plce, no wrn.*

This is a code he cannot crack. He closes the phone, lays it face down where he found it. He closes his eyes, too, and thinks now the sound of the rain might carry him off, float him along more gently than a flooding river. But once more, rising from his stomach, comes a bubble of noxious gas from the ground-up root that's supposed to help him sleep. He burps and stares into the darkness overhead.

24. THE GIFT

HER FAVORITE TREE IS a mile up the river trail, just before it makes its first switchback and begins rising to a rocky bluff overlooking rapids. She drags her father there three weeks in a row in late winter, though the steep incline—including a set of stone stairs that seem as if they were made for a giant's stride—challenges his lower back. The tree is a dozen yards off the trail, a brief scramble over rocks and fallen logs. He's breathing hard when they reach it. Still, he hasn't complained, at least not vocally. He seems to understand how much these outings matter to her, though that, too, she hasn't said out loud.

Whenever she visits, she has a little ritual: first to circle the tree three times, then to tap a knuckle against each of its largest visible roots where they emerge from the trunk. This alone takes a few minutes, because the tree is enormous—an ancient western red cedar her father says could be more than five hundred years old. They can live to fifteen hundred years, he says, outlasting by centuries the Douglas firs that shade them. This one is hollow in the middle with a small opening she can climb through if she contorts her body to the side and then twists her shoulders to pull her hips through. Once inside, she can stand all the way up. The space is wide enough that her arms don't touch the sides. The only light comes from the notch she crawled through, which now seems too small for her, down at her ankles. Normally she might be scared of spiders—she doesn't mind them when she can see them but hates the idea of them dropping into her hair—but for some reason, when she's inside the tree, she feels protected from them and from just about everything else. It's dry in here even though outside it's drizzling; her father reminds her several times as he stands guard out front, shuffling his feet and occasionally jogging in place to keep warm.

"I told you to wear your rain gear," she says, but she's in no hurry to come out. This is the most important part of the visit. She reaches a hand over her head, stretches onto her toes until she can feel a little notch in the wood, a shelf maybe two inches deep and four inches wide. When she confirms it's empty, she slips a hand into a jacket pocket and pulls out a small package, wrapped in tissue and tied with twine. Inside is a shell she found on the beach some years ago—a limpet, she thinks—along with a note written in the smallest handwriting she can manage. She spent the morning writing it, explaining where the shell came from, what sort of creature had once lived in it, and what it's like to stare out at the ocean and see nothing but water and sky meeting at the horizon. The tree has been here since Shakespeare was alive, her father has told her, and might live another thousand years after she's gone, but it'll never see the ocean, which makes her a little sad. But it's also the kind of sadness she likes to indulge by lingering in it for as long as possible, and though she hates writing papers for school, feels as if every word she gets out follows a process of unendurable torture, the note came easily and gave her a surprising hour of pleasure.

She doesn't believe in God, at least not the way kids at school talk about it, or her bubby, who refers to Hashem. The idea of some big divine dude in the sky who made everything and judges her for her deeds is something she finds ridiculous, and she's not shy about saying so; one of her oldest friends, Kelly, whom she met at Small World Montessori when they were four, has stopped speaking to her because apparently it's impossible to be friends with someone you know is going to hell.

But she hasn't told any of them what she does believe, which is that this tree receives her gifts, reads her notes, knows her, and appreciates her visits. If it lives another thousand years, it will remember her, she thinks, because she has been willing to spend time with it while everyone else just hurries by on the trail.

She's too embarrassed to say any of this to her friends at school and hasn't even told her father what she does in here, except to say that she likes being inside the tree, that it makes her feel more connected to nature, which is something he wants her to feel, though he has no suggestions about how to do so other than fly-fishing, which looks to her like the most boring activity ever invented. She first left a treasure last fall, a gold-plated bracelet with multicolor glass beads her Grandma Norgrove had given her for her last birthday; she didn't like wearing it because it was too loose on her wrist, though she thought it was pretty enough. She set it on the narrow shelf thinking she'd retrieve it the next time she came back. But when she returned earlier this month, it was gone. So that time she left an agate she'd found on the riverbank, fat and smoothly polished, and a week later that, too, had disappeared. And now every week she returns with a new gift, and each time the tree—or the spirit who lives in it—has claimed the last.

She slips the wrapped shell and note onto the shelf, presses a hand to the inner bark, thinks she feels warmth coming from the tree, though maybe it's only from her own skin. Then she crouches and wiggles out of the notch, feet first. Her father, hair wet and pushed back from his forehead, blows into his hands and rubs them together.

"Can we go?" he says. "Smells over here."

"Smells?"

"Someone used this recently," he says and gestures to a stump a few feet away, where a wad of toilet paper is disintegrating into the soil.

"Here?" she says.

"You think you're the only one who comes this way?"

"Why would they do it next to the tree?"

"They think it's far enough from the trail. We're not the brightest species, you know."

"You think someone else goes inside too?" she asks, staring at the dark triangle of the opening—the secret entrance, she wants to believe, to another world.

"This is one of the most popular trails in the state," he says. "You didn't think you were the only one, did you?"

25. REVENGE

HE HASN'T BEEN HOME for several days, so the place is a disaster when they arrive. The scraps of his dinner from Tuesday—instant rice, canned chili—still decorate the dining table, along with a T-shirt and a pair of boxers at the base of the stairs, muddy boots and work gloves just inside the sliding door to the deck, a book face down on the couch where he was reading when he got the call from Maggie. He began preparing Sills for the mess ahead of time, as soon as he picked her up, and he continues to justify it as he scrambles to clean up and keep her from wondering what prevented him from doing so earlier in the week. "Just crazy busy at work the last few days," he says. "Didn't get home before ten and out the door at seven. Project's almost done, though. Won't be this way next week."

She doesn't ask any questions but looks at him skeptically. He knows why: he can't hide the giddy exhilaration that ripples through his body and flushes his face, can't tame the smile he's worn to work the last three days, which his coworkers, too, clearly noted without comment, though he's sure they've been gossiping among themselves.

And the reason? He's getting laid! *I got laid last night*, he thought Wednesday morning, and Thursday morning, and again this morning. His nerves are on fire with the unspoken words, from the soles of his feet to his scalp. And of course his dick, too, though what he feels most there is simply the call of desire—*more, more, more*—as if three nights of sliding in and out of Maggie V. after a year of isolation and sad masturbation weren't enough to satisfy it, as if it could only be content being in the grip of her soft, wet spaces and nowhere else.

Magdalena Valente. A name synonymous with sweaty bodies and heaving breath. They'd dated years ago, long before he'd met Veronica, back when he first moved to Portland in his early twenties and spent every night packed into a music club, ears assaulted by exquisitely loud guitars: Trans Am at La Luna, Hazel at Satyricon, Dead Moon at the Twilight Café. Maggie was always there, tiny and sleek, an Italian spitfire with black bangs and muscled arms, named after a Biblical harlot with a heart of gold. So many nights rolling around with her on his mattress on the floor of a basement in Southeast, or in her bungalow near Alberta when the neighborhood was only just beginning to squeeze out its longtime Black residents with refurbished houses and rising property taxes. He was blind to such sinister undercurrents then, swept up as he was in the innocence of youthful thrills. Now, even all these years later, the memory of that time remains sticky with passion and sweetened alcohol and betrayal. It took him a few months to learn she was rolling in other sheets, too, and that she made the same noises in other ears. "I'm not built for one person at a time," she'd told him when he objected. "I've got too much love to give."

After that, Lewis couldn't help feeling he was getting only a fraction of what Maggie had to offer, and he wanted all or nothing. Though at the time letting her go made him weep, whatever regret he experienced then had long since faded into bittersweet nostalgia. Mostly he was grateful he hadn't gotten herpes from her, as one of his friends did a year or so later.

Now, though? He's happy to take whatever scraps she might toss his way. He'll take his chances with herpes, too, though on the way to her house he stopped at Walgreens, bought the largest box of condoms he could find, insisted on using them even though she'd had her tubes tied after her second child was born. Despite her wild youth, she was the first of the crowd he ran with then to settle down, marrying the bass player in a band whose shows Lewis had seen a few times out of obligation to mutual friends—a mediocre power pop trio whose songs he was glad never to have to hear again—and promptly getting pregnant. Her youngest had just started college. He'd stayed in touch with her only in the most casual way; they'd see each other at gatherings old friends arranged from time to time, a backyard barbecue, a reunion show of some band they'd once admired, now a bunch of middle-aged guys with receding hairlines strumming on a makeshift stage. He spent less time at these events talking to Maggie than to her husband, who now worked for a big mortgage firm and wore loafers with collapsible backs. He kept up with her on Facebook, knew when her kids graduated middle school and then high school, knew when she had a bout with breast cancer, caught early enough that she only had a lump removed, no mastectomy or chemo.

Now he has access to Facebook only at work, and since his split with Veronica, he mostly avoids it; he doesn't want images of people's happy lives taunting him all day. But after not having opened it for weeks, boredom with his job brought him back, and he was surprised to find a message from Maggie waiting for him. She was sorry to hear about his divorce, she said. She wanted him to know even if it felt impossible now, he'd recover, he was a super guy and had a lot of good years ahead of him. From her recent posts he could see she was still married to the bass-player-turned-mortgage-broker, that she'd gained some weight but still wore that sly, seductive look whenever someone snapped a photo of her. He thanked her, said it was easier being single at forty-six than it had been at twenty-three. *Now that the blood doesn't flow south so often*, he added, and immediately felt stupid when he pressed return. She wrote back, *There are pills for that, you know.* And he, *I'll have to check with my cardiologist.*

Their flirtation went on this way for a few weeks, during which Maggie made it clear that she and her husband enjoyed an open relationship of sorts: not with any regularity or particular ground rules, just some playing around from time to time, especially when he was away on business trips. During one exchange she asked for his number, and he gave her both, letting her know his cell phone didn't have service on nights and weekends. He expected her to text him titillating messages while he was at work, maybe even a suggestive photo or two. Instead, she called his landline after ten on a Tuesday. When he picked up, she said without waiting for him to speak, "I just dropped him off at the airport. House is empty till Sunday."

He drove the dark country roads and the bright freeway and city streets that were both familiar and always slightly different than he remembered and arrived just after midnight. Only then did he wonder if he'd locked the cabin and turned down the heat and shut off the stove. But it was too late to worry about any of that. Because now there was nothing but Maggie. Maggie at the front door, greeting him in a satin robe. Maggie on the couch. Maggie against the kitchen counter. Maggie bent over the bed,

Maggie's mouth, Maggie's glistening labia, Maggie asleep and
snoring beside him.

And the sex itself? It was good. That's what he would have
said to anyone who asked. Not great, but how could it be after
so long? And had it really been so great twenty-three years
ago? Probably not. Because great sex was sex with Veronica,
even when it was routine, even when they were distracted,
even when they were fighting. Yes, he enjoyed fucking Maggie,
but he was aware the whole time that she didn't grab his butt
just before she came the way Veronica did, that she talked too
much when he was trying to concentrate on not finishing too
soon, that she always wanted to switch to a new position just
as he was getting into a groove with the last one. It was good
fun, it kept his mind off his losses, though oddly Veronica was
more present in his thoughts than she'd been in months. The
strangest thing was how little he thought about Sills for those
three days, though he still remembered to text her during his
lunch hour—*miss you kiddo* and *let me know what you want for
dinners this wkend, going to the store tomrrw*—and how quickly
he settled back into his old neighborhood in Portland, where
there was a new French bakery and a bar that specialized in
Scandinavian cocktails.

Still, he was relieved to be picking up Sills and heading
back to the woods on Friday afternoon, to reconnect with the
life he'd abandoned in such a frenzy. Maggie, however, was irritated when he left that morning. "He's gone two more days,"
she said. "I don't want to waste them." When he said he was
sorry, he couldn't miss any time with his daughter, she yanked
up her underwear and said with a cruelty that both surprised
him and confirmed what he realized he should have expected
all along, "Guess I'll have to see who else is around."

Now, scraping dried-out beans and rice into the compost

bin, starting water to boil as Sills finds a bag of tortilla chips to fill up on before he can finish cooking, he wonders if the whole thing was a mistake. He's glad to have satisfied a craving, to have put to rest the thought that he's missing out on the most important things in life, but the feeling he's left with isn't fulfillment. Not regret, either, not exactly, but a sickening kind of emptiness. The exhilarating flush is receding, and the giddiness too. All that remains is the vague desire, the bottomless longing, an itch in his crotch, an ache in his abdominal muscles and hamstrings from repeated movements he hasn't made in so long.

He checks his voice mail. There are several messages. The first from Maggie on Wednesday morning. She must have left it just after he walked out her door. "Can't wait till you come back tonight," she says. "I'm dripping just thinking about it." The second from Veronica, letting him know the dates she'll be away next month, visiting her brother in Los Angeles, extra days he'll have to wake early to get Sills to school on time. Then another from Maggie, left this morning, her tone somewhat conciliatory, somewhat chiding, mostly just cold. "Sorry you can't stay here and play this weekend. He'll be away again in June. For a full week, if you want to plan ahead."

The last message features a voice he doesn't recognize, or rather, one he recognizes but can't place—not until it calls back to mind a jaunty bass line, silly lyrics delivered with sarcasm, a song he hated twenty years ago. Only now the voice, still resonant and slightly nasal, is brittle with anger and outrage and perhaps a hint of heartache. "Thanks, man," Maggie's husband says. "You really did me a solid. Just when we were finally getting past all that shit. Goddamn. I know I screwed up. But did you really have to help her get back at me? I thought we were friends."

Were we? Lewis wonders as the message cuts off. Has he ever really been friends with anyone?

"You want a rematch tonight?" Sills asks through the corner of her mouth not pinched around a tortilla chip. She holds up the chess board and the black king. "Try to get even? Or maybe you're afraid I'll checkmate your ass again."

26. HAMSA

THIS TIME HE DOES everything right. He remembers to call on
the actual date, early in the day, and says she has his permission
to skip school if she wants, though of course his permission
doesn't matter on a Tuesday when she's at home with her
mother. Plus, she has a quiz in her Spanish class, one she's
studied for, and she doesn't want to postpone it. But afterward,
her mother takes her and three of her friends up to Portland to
go roller-skating at Oaks Park, where they fall and laugh a lot—
all except June, who's now officially a jammer on the Salem
roller derby team and spends the whole night showing off her
backward crossovers. Skye has such a good time that she almost
forgets she'll have another birthday celebration three days later.
It strikes her only when she sees her father's car already in the
parking lot when she gets out of ballet on Friday. There's a
wrapped box on the passenger seat. "This is just a teaser," he
says. "There are more when we get home."

The box is narrow on one side, long on the other, and when

she tears the paper away and opens it, she's not surprised to find a necklace inside. But she is surprised by the pendant at the end of the silver chain, a little hand made of blue and white glass, fingers pointing down, an eye in the palm's center. It's beautiful and a little strange, and she instantly loves it, though she doesn't know what it is. She doesn't think she wants to know, either, but before she can say anything, her father tells her it's called a *hamsa*, and that it's an ancient Jewish symbol. "Arabic too. Pretty much all over the Middle East. Probably goes back to the Mesopotamians. My grandparents used to have one on the wall of their living room."

"What's it mean?" she asks.

"I would have gotten you a Star of David, but that's too loaded these days," he says while pulling out of the parking lot. He's heading in the opposite direction from usual, not toward downtown and the road that will take them toward the mountains. "Now everyone thinks it means you support the Israeli government. Thought about a Chai too. I like that because it means life, but it's also the number eighteen, and I don't know, it seems weird to give someone an eighteen for their thirteenth birthday. Anyway, I thought you should have something Jewy, since if I weren't the bad son and father your bubby tells me I am, you might have had a bat mitzvah this year."

She clips the chain around her neck, and the hand dangles at her throat. "What's it mean?" she asks again.

"It's protection," he says. "Wards off the evil eye."

"Evil eye?"

"Curses."

"Jews believe in curses?"

"I guess so," he says as they turn in to the lot of her favorite restaurant, one he almost ruined for her a few years ago when he said there was no decent pasta in Salem, hardly any in all of Oregon, and that one day he'd take her to New Jersey so she could learn how marinara was supposed to taste. Her mother must have scolded him afterward because later he apologized and admitted he'd been a jerk, but for months she refused whenever he offered to take her back. Now he says nothing about their different understanding of al dente or the proper amount of oregano in a sauce, just finds a spot to park close to the entrance and says he hopes she's as hungry as he is, because he plans to order appetizers and dessert.

"What sort of curses?" she asks, fingering the pendant as the host seats them at a table near the windows, where she can gaze across the whole dining room, a crowded space full of loud people talking over loud jazz, waiters in black turtlenecks hurrying through with steaming dishes. It's still her favorite restaurant, even if the pasta is mediocre as her father once said. She can't wait to eat it, a big pile of twirly red noodles with heaps of parmesan on top.

"The passive-aggressive kind, I suppose," he says. "The ones you don't see coming. Just a sideways glance, and your sheep stop producing milk."

"Can anyone do it?" She glances around at the people eating and talking. No one's looking her way—not now, at least.

"Good question," he says. "Maybe you need some evil eye training. I wish my bubby was still alive so I could ask her. If there was anyone in my family who would have cursed people, it was her."

"It's kind of horrifying," she says. "You're just minding your own business, and someone looks at you and wrecks your whole life?"

"She didn't trust anyone. Used to accuse her neighbor

of stealing her newspaper all the time. That's why you need the hamsa."

"I mean, kids at school would destroy each other. None of us would still be standing."

"Probably you've got to be an adult before you get your cursing powers. Learn to be responsible with them first."

"Don't Jews believe you're an adult at thirteen?"

"True. You might be ready."

"Everybody better watch out," she says.

He smiles, a little uneasily. After the server takes their order, she peeks around the room again. Still, no one seems to be glancing her way, but she feels eyes on her all the same. There's no one she recognizes in the restaurant, though a woman three tables over seems vaguely familiar. Maybe she's the mother of a kid at school, or maybe she's a teacher Skye hasn't yet had. She doesn't like the look of her, in any case, younger than her father but double-chinned, with a sour expression and an icy stiffness to the way she lifts her fork and chews silently as the man across from her mutters a few words Skye can't make out. She cuts a look at the woman and thinks, *May your noodles be overcooked, your sauce too herby.* When she turns back, she catches a flash of the blue and white hand below her chin, its eye taking in everything she can't see.

Her father says, "I can't believe I have a teenager."

"Believe it," she says. "Or you'll be sorry."

SPRING

27. LOCAL

LAST WEEK IT HAPPENED in the liquor store on the highway, and now again in the little grocery in downtown Millburg (though the word *downtown* seems like a stretch to describe two commercial blocks in a village of fewer than two thousand residents): the clerk greets him by name. Regulars at the tavern, along with its two bartenders, have been doing so for weeks. He's been here long enough now to be considered part of the terrain, a true inhabitant of the canyon rather than one of the thousands who pass through without giving it more than a glance, or the hundreds who fish or paddle the river and quickly return to their homes in the valley. He takes pride in the fact, though what exactly gives him pride, he isn't sure: that he has lasted so long out here, that the commute hasn't yet broken him, that he can claim a small piece of this place no one else seems to want?

The post office clerk has been calling him by name the longest, though she has the advantage of seeing it on his packages.

She's a sturdy woman in her early sixties, with gray hair pinned at her neck and reading glasses propped on her head. When she returns from the back room with his mail—the few items too large to fit in his PO box—she gestures to the front window, behind which Sills is standing with one hand deep in her pockets. "Remind me your kid's name again?" When he tells her, she says, "Right. Skye. Pretty girl."

The way she says it suggests that, unlike Lewis, Sills isn't yet a local. Her hair, recently dyed purple at the tips, makes her stand out, as does the designer rain jacket Veronica's parents recently bought her, the rubber boots that come up nearly to her knees. The hand not in her pocket is holding a book—a graphic novel with a brightly colored cover—and that, too, sets her apart from the people rolling past in pickup trucks.

"Bright too," the clerk says. "You planning to send her to the high school here?"

Lewis explains his situation, expecting the clerk to judge him for his choices, to tell him about the dangers of raising kids in a city—even a modestly sized one like Salem—and the benefits of small-town life and country air on a growing body and mind.

Instead she says, "Smart choice. School here's terrible. They can't keep teachers for more than a year or two. Except the bad ones."

Lewis thanks her, glances at Sills through the window. Her posture is awful, he thinks, spine curved, head bent low over the book's pages. One day she'll have back problems just like her father.

"Lewis," the clerk says and pauses, as if to linger over his name, the strange sound of its syllables almost nonsensical in her gruff voice. "This place is dying. Has been for a long time.

When I was a kid here in the sixties, there was money at least. Plenty of timber, shifts at the mill for anyone who wanted them. Now it's just bleak. The kids here grow up learning to hate everything. Tourists. Kayaks. The trees that used to be their parents' livelihood. They'd burn the whole thing down if they could. You know what most of our business is in here, most of the mail I sort? Prescriptions. Pain pills people don't need. Or didn't need until they started taking them. Now they can't do without."

This speech sounds rehearsed, as if she's been waiting for the right moment to deliver it. And by the time she finishes, she's staring at the window again. When he follows her gaze, he sees that this time Sills is looking up from her book and her mouth is moving. He can't see who she's talking to, but from a dozen feet away her eyes seem guarded, her stance squared. Not as hardened as she might be if he'd raised her in a big city but at least without the oblivious openness that came from a suburban childhood like his own.

"I guess you got a good setup there on the river," the clerk says. "It must be peaceful. And a nice place for the kid on weekends. But to be honest, I don't know what you're doing up here. Longer you stay, the more it sucks you under."

The door opens and in steps a young man Lewis recognizes, square-jawed and scruffy, wearing waterproof pants and filthy boots. He can't be more than thirty. Lewis has seen him in the tavern a few times and knows he's a raft guide. He runs the operation that floats novices down the class-two rapids all summer. He says hello but doesn't know Lewis's name, nor does Lewis know his. But Lewis admires his healthy gait, his carefree smile. Despite what the postal clerk says, here's a local who isn't despairing, doesn't believe the place is on its last breath.

He's the future of the canyon, one Lewis wants to be part of for as long as he can.

"Franny trying to scare you away?" the raft guide asks. "She's been working on me for years."

"And you know I'm right," the clerk says.

"Don't listen to her," the raft guide says. "She's just trying to drive property values down. Wants to invest in vacation rentals."

"I'm not going anywhere," Lewis says.

"Your funeral," the clerk says.

"That your kid out there?" the raft guide asks. "Cool hair."

Lewis wishes them a good afternoon. When he steps out, Sills closes her book around a finger. "Who was that guy?" she asks.

"You think he's hot, don't you."

She makes a disgusted face—a sincere one, no coyness or embarrassment in it—and shakes her head. "He asked if I like to party," she says. "And told me how to find his trailer. He thought I was in college."

Through the window, he watches the clerk head into the backroom. When she does, the raft guide leans over the counter and fishes in a plastic bin. If he finds anything he's looking for, Lewis can't tell. When the clerk returns, he shoves his hands in his pockets.

"We shouldn't come into town so often," Lewis says and waves the envelopes the clerk handed him in the direction of the cabin. "Not like there's much in the mail worth looking at."

28. AUTOPILOT

"I DON'T HAVE ANY excuse," he says. "I had it right there on my calendar. In my phone too."

He's been apologizing all weekend, and she's been telling him it's no big deal, she doesn't care, it was only a stupid parent-teacher night, and her mom was there, so it's not like she felt abandoned or anything. If he should apologize to anyone, it should be to his ex-wife, who cursed him out the whole drive home while Skye did her best to defend him, or at least to calm her mother down, saying they were lucky to have the conferences without him, because he would have spent the whole time trying to make jokes to keep the teachers from saying anything negative about her. They hadn't said much negative anyway—after falling behind before the holidays, she'd caught up in her language arts class, her favorite, and she's managed to get by in algebra, though the sight of numbers combined with letters instantly makes her yawn.

She might have gotten a bad report in social science, her least-favorite subject: she often drifts off during lessons, doodling or studying the back-of-the-head cowlicks of the boy who sits in front of her. But her teacher's a ditz who only wants everyone to like her, and she told her mother Skye is a delight to have in her class, that she always surprises her with her insights, especially when they're discussing civics and the country's democratic institutions. Skye supposed she was referring to the time she repeated what her mother had said about the electoral college being a racist system created to protect slavery, which made the teacher glance at the open classroom door before hurrying them on to another topic. Now she said to Skye's mother, "She's quiet but spirited. I think she'd make a strong debater if she wants to try out when she gets to high school."

Skye would rather step on glass and swim with sharks than join the debate team, which her mother knew without her having to say anything; her mother smiled politely and thanked the teacher for her work and, when they were alone again, said, "Some people need to try out a few different careers before they find the right one." Skye's mother, who now worked as an advocate for seniors and people with disabilities in the state's Department of Health and Human Services, had waited tables for several years even though she knew she was terrible at it. "I could pretend to be nice most of the time," she said. "But if people were rude to me, I'd purposely screw up their order five different ways." Then, with obvious pride, she added, "There were more complaints about me than any other server."

Her father, on the other hand, would have gushed over the idea of Skye on the debate team, at least in front of the teacher. He would have asked too many questions about how she could sign up and what she needed to do to prepare, and Skye would have gritted her teeth and felt her ears burning the whole time. So why would she have wanted him in the room?

"I should have been there," he says now, hanging up their

wet jackets on a clothesline he's strung up over the woodstove. It's only five o'clock but so dark with clouds and steady rain it seems as if dusk has already arrived. They only managed a fifteen-minute walk up the road, which was so full of puddles they jumped more than stepped, before giving up and coming home. "You've got two parents who care about your education. Your teachers should know that."

"I told them you were sick," she says, though in truth she didn't mention him at all, and none of the teachers asked.

"I had every intention of going. I told your mom I'd meet you in the auditorium."

"Syphilis," she says, naming the most disgusting disease she learned about in her mortifying sex ed class, taught by a stocky female gym teacher and volleyball coach who never cracked a smile and made each student come up to the front of the room and point out some part of their anatomy on a rubber model. Skye had to do the uterus, which was obvious and boring. June got the clitoris and made a big show of twirling her finger before pressing the spot. Even then the teacher only stared at them all grimly before describing the various ways you could die from having sex.

"But the thing is," her father says, as if he hasn't heard, "I get into this kind of robotic routine during the week." He adds more wood to the fire, pokes it with a long barbecue skewer because he never remembers to buy a set of proper hearth tools. "Like autopilot. Get up, make lunch, go to work, drive home. It's like my brain can't accommodate anything else."

"It's because of the bacteria," she says, sprawling on the couch. "Little spirals that screw into your cells."

"I was all the way here when I realized. If I turned around and went back, I would have missed it anyway."

"Antibiotics are effective," she says. "Most cases clear up within a month."

"It's like I'm asleep all week, or hypnotized. I only really wake up when I pick you up on Friday. That's when my actual life starts up again."

"It's a little more complicated since you're allergic to penicillin. But there are alternatives."

"Anyway," he says, stripping off his socks and hanging them over the line. "I'm really sorry. You must have been pissed. And rightly so."

"If you don't treat it, it'll get into your brain," she says, struggling now to remember specifics from the class and instead making up whatever sounds most horrific. "You start to hallucinate and think people are chasing after you with daggers. You'll believe you can fly and jump out a window. And if that doesn't kill you, then you start bleeding out your ears."

He looks up at her then and blinks, as if he's just snapped out of a deep trance. "What the hell are you talking about?" he asks.

"Never do it again," she says.

29. PUSSY

THE RIVER IS HIGH after a quick spring snowmelt, the current strong against his legs, and even with hip waders on, Lewis steps out only up to his knees. He has a solid rock shelf beneath him, and he adjusts his feet into a wide stance to give himself more leverage. He has no interest in getting swept downstream and drowning in the clear, frigid water like the fool everyone believes him to be—Veronica, his parents and sister, his coworkers who like to joke that one day he'll show up to the office wearing nothing but bearskin. Sills is behind him on the stony beach, which is narrow at this time of year but bordered on two sides by a calm, shallow pool in which she safely turns over rocks to look for crawdads. Still, he reminds her every few minutes to take care, watch her step, make sure she's aware of her footing.

His friend Alexander, on the other hand, is upriver a dozen yards and in the water all the way to his waist. Lewis knows the spot well enough to picture what's under his feet, a bed of loose rocks worn smooth by thousands of years in the current, slippery with algae. One wrong step and his waders will fill with water.

Alexander—who goes by the confusing nickname *Zander* rather than *Alex*—isn't someone Lewis knows particularly well. Their wives were in a yoga class together when they were both pregnant, and the four of them went out to dinner every couple of months; twice, their families took weekend trips together to the beach, during which Zander bragged about catching chinook and steelhead the previous season and mocked Lewis for his handful of trout. Lewis expected the friendship to end with his marriage, but Zander surprised him by calling regularly after the separation, checking up on him, offering to take him out for a beer after work. Lewis occasionally accepted out of loneliness and the need for distraction, but the truth is he's never much enjoyed Zander's company. He's a large man, broad-shouldered and thick through the middle, and he likes to tell people everything he knows about subjects in which he's far from expert. Years ago, when he heard Lewis majored in English, he listed all the reasons Larry McMurtry was the best writer America had ever known, and when Lewis tried to argue—not because he cared much, but because he thought sparking debate was the point of such an assertion—Zander clammed up, offended, it seemed, that Lewis would try to posit an opinion.

It was Zander's idea to come out and see the place and cast a few flies. He didn't give Lewis a chance to object, though when Lewis told Sills about the impending visit, he made it sound as if he were the one to do the inviting. She just squinted and said, "I thought you hated that guy." She'd just gotten her braces off, and the expansive whiteness of her teeth surprised him every time she opened her mouth. It was as if she'd matured a whole year in the days since he'd last seen her, and her words, like her teeth, had been stripped of any childhood naivete.

"I don't hate anyone," he responded, which wasn't true at all—he could list a dozen people without a moment's hesitation—though his feelings about Zander were more complicated. Despite his aggression, his arrogance, his touchiness, loyalty counted for something.

Now Zander calls to him, "You'll never get a bite that far back. Rainbows run the middle this time of year."

He doesn't know if that's accurate or not and suspects Zander has no idea what he's talking about. But catching fish is less important to him than staying upright and keeping his balls from freezing. "Bottom's real slick over there," he calls back. "Wouldn't try to move around too much."

"Don't be such a pussy," Zander calls back. Behind him, Sills lets out a snorting laugh. The phrase doesn't surprise him as much as the feeling it inspires: not injury or anger but nostalgia. It's been many years—decades—since he's heard those words directed at him, but he was on the receiving end plenty while growing up in New Jersey in the 1980s, when boys who didn't perform a certain style of masculinity—sporty or sadistic—were either pussies or faggots. He was sometimes called the latter, though by the time he hit puberty, at which point he spent much of his time in school hiding erections and his time alone pulling on them, he was quite clear about his preference for women.

Was he a pussy? He shied away from a kickball beamed at his head, he didn't stand up for himself when some lunkhead grabbed his copy of *The Dark Knight Returns* and wouldn't give it back, and he could never get up the nerve to ask a girl to dance at a junior high social. But the word itself always confused him.

He was a fan of cats, for one, and rather than timid or docile, he thought of them as unpredictable and mysterious, sometimes affectionate, sometimes fierce. And even more mysterious were the images he saw in dirty magazines boys passed around on the playground, which he also associated with brief glimpses up classmates' legs, when skirts parted to reveal triangles of white or blue or pink fabric.

Before he can stop himself, he replies with the comeback he learned in those far-off days, one always guaranteed to shut up whoever flung the word his way: "You are what you eat."

But as soon as he's spoken, he regrets it, just as he regrets letting Zander invite himself over to fish in the river he pretends to understand better than Lewis, even though Lewis is the one to spend every day beside it, studying its movements and moods. He glances over his shoulder. Sills scrunches up her face, as if she's gotten a whiff of something foul, upper lip pulled back from straightened teeth—a look of pure revulsion. He gives her a smirk and a shrug, but she turns back to the shallows, continuing her search for pincers and antennae.

His words have the desired effect on Zander, however, who responds with a forced laugh, stiff with insult, and begins a new cast. His form is sloppy. He reaches too far back on each swing, and when he finally releases, the fly lands only a few feet in front of him. He gets himself off-balance in the process and takes a step forward. The water bobs up to the top of his waders. *This is it*, Lewis thinks: the moment he'll prove himself to be a pussy, watching and doing nothing as his friend—yes, despite everything, Zander is one of the best friends he has— gets sucked under.

But Zander recovers, retreats a few steps toward the bank. The water line is back at his waist. Lewis thinks of Verlaine licking his tail, of triangles of fabric, of tangles of hair and the folds of flesh behind them, where he likes to press his nose and explore with his tongue. If only he could be so powerful, so mysterious. He tosses his fly into the current and watches it float downstream. Nothing strikes. If anything beneath the surface is interested in what he has to offer, for now it takes a pass.

30. THE KISS

HER FATHER LIES IMMOBILE on the couch with a bag of ice under his lower back, so she heads out to the river on her own. "Check in every once in a while," he calls after her. "So I know you haven't fallen in."

"And if I don't? You're gonna dive in and fish me out? You can't even stand up."

She tells herself she's bored, but that's not really true. She has plenty to keep her busy. She gets to work right away making little boats out of fresh osoberry leaves, tying the ends with dried blades of last year's grass. The water is high enough that all she has to do is toss them from the bank, and they land in an eddy, twirl a couple of times, and zip downstream. She knows they won't make it all the way to the Willamette, much less to the Pacific, but she likes to imagine them in the ocean anyway, heading out with the tide, riding waves, dodging the beaks of pecking gulls, rising up on the backs of migrating gray whales when they breach.

The thought momentarily distracts her from others that have been bothering her all week—particularly those involving how she behaves around her friends, always accommodating them rather than asserting her own desires. On the playground, she wants to join the game of capture the flag they played in the fall and all last year, but June has decided capture the flag is lame because you can't knock people over the way she does in roller derby, and Lizzy doesn't want to play because she's afraid of getting her jeans muddy, and Kendall is chunky and out of shape and embarrassed when she's forced to run. So instead they sit on the concrete pad above the soccer field, talking about other people's crushes—never their own—and guessing whether or not any of the few official couples among their classmates have done more than kiss.

Since Skye hasn't kissed anyone yet, "more than" doesn't mean much to her. She understands the mechanics of sex and the various ways people can give each other pleasure—her mother explained it all to her, in excruciating detail, when she was nine or ten. But she hasn't gotten over the idea of putting her mouth against someone else's, pressing lips—or worse, tongues—and sharing breath. The part she has the hardest time imagining is pulling away and looking into another person's eyes after you've just exchanged spit and not bursting into laughter. That's what scares her most: that when she finally does kiss a boy, she'll ruin it all by laughing in his face. She wants to ask her friends about the possibility, especially June, who claims she's kissed three people—two boys and one girl. But the real problem is that she doesn't trust her friends to keep her confidence; the moment after she asks the question, they'll spread it all over the school. That's what bothers her most as she makes her boats out of leaves and sends them to swim with the whales.

But now she's distracted all over again by anger at her friends, and even more at herself for putting up with them, and she throws the next boat too hard. It catches air, lifts, flips over, and lands face down in the rushing water. And just as it does, she spots another boat, a real one, dash around the bend upstream. A kayak, bright orange, moving fast. It's early in the season to run this part of the river, which stays dangerous until midsummer. Even for experts, it's dicey now. The paddler is wearing a helmet and wetsuit, she can see that even as he first appears around the boulder on the opposite bank, and when he heads into the rapids, the kayak bucks down and then quickly up, turns sideways, and rolls. It happens so fast only afterward does she realize she hasn't taken a breath. She's ready to run into the house to call her dad, who'd be useless with his pulled muscle and pinched nerve, so maybe she'd call 911, though if there were really an emergency, no one could possibly get here in time. But the kayak rolls back upright, the rider pumps his paddle on the left side, and then he's past the rapids and into deeper water, which moves quickly but without obstacles. When he comes near, Skye shouts, "You're crazy!"

She can't see his face well, only a hunk of wet hair pressed to his forehead; a narrow, smooth chin; and lots of teeth. He waves and calls back, "You only die once!"

And then, before she knows what she's doing, she presses two fingers to her lips and blows him a kiss. She thinks it's the strangest thing she's ever done and can't wait to tell her friends, though afterward they're guaranteed to talk about it behind her back. She doesn't care if everyone knows. The paddler presses a hand to his chest, then twirls the paddle over his head. She does laugh then and thinks it's exactly the right thing to do. It doesn't ruin anything. She watches until the kayak reaches the next set of rapids, a hundred yards downstream, where he plunges his paddle into the water, turns sharply, and disappears from view.

When she goes back inside, her father yells, "Where the hell have you been?"

"You don't really think I'd fall in, do you? I'm not a toddler."

"I need help here!"

Most of the ice has melted, and the plastic bag has broken open. He's soaking wet from the middle of his back to his thighs. The helpless look he turns on her is so ridiculous she has to turn away. She hurries to the closet for towels, mops him as best she can, helps him stand so he can limp to the bathroom. The laughter is still bubbling in her, but she manages to keep it inside until he closes the door. When she hears the shower running, she lets it out in a quick, rattling shudder that no longer sounds funny, nor is the feeling that comes with its eruption quite joyful, though she's breathing hard when she finishes, nearly spent, bending over with hands on knees.

31. THE SCAR

A WILDFIRE SCORCHED THIS part of the forest a year and a half earlier, burning through downfall and stumps and dry underbrush and leaving a blackened floor. Most of the bigger trees survived, and now some of the ferns are recovering, but it's still a bleak landscape of cinder and char, with branches creaking precariously overhead and dry hemlock needles covering everything. They have to step carefully so as not to fall into ankle-twisting holes where ancient roots burned away. "Why'd you bring me here?" Sills asks, though she already knows the answer. Last year Lewis found a handful of black morels growing near a singed trunk, and now they're here with two backpacks and a dozen plastic take-out containers, hoping for a haul.

Nothing excited him more than finding those little brain-shaped fungus blooms a year ago during the height of his grief, and nothing has excited him more than the possibility of returning and finding more, and having Sills with him when he does.

He knows she's unnerved by the look of a burned forest, but he's reminded her on multiple occasions that fires are a necessary part of the natural cycle, especially smaller ones like this that don't destroy the old growth: they provide nutrients for the soil; they keep smaller trees from being outcompeted; they prevent more intense fires by clearing away fuel; and of course they stimulate morels, which grow in secret for years underground, to send up their delectable fruits to spore and make his mouth water.

"Some trees need fire in order to even sprout," he says. "Lodgepole pine cones? They only open after a burn. Sit on the ground for decades, waiting until the Doug firs get cleared away so they have a chance at some sunlight."

"You told me already," she says, crawling across a blackened log that crunches under her knees and covers her palms with soot. "Like, a hundred times."

Of course she has good reason to be unnerved, because while everything he said is true, drought and the warming climate mean far more frequent and bigger fires than are healthy for anyone. Since he moved to Oregon twenty-three years ago, he's seen stretches of his favorite areas burned to nothing. He tries not to think too much about what that will mean in the future, whether the woods they love will be here for Sills to enjoy with her kids should she have them. It helps to have treasure to search for in the wreckage. Last year, he made himself a morel-sherry cream sauce to go over gnocchi, reverse-engineered from a dish he and Veronica shared years ago at a beach restaurant that no longer exists. This time he ate it by himself with a glass of cheap pinot noir, and though it was the best thing he'd tasted for months, he sobbed before taking the last bite.

Now he wants Sills to taste it, in part because he knows

how much she'll enjoy it, in part to give him a new association
with the flavor that haunts him—something other than a beach
motel with a gas fireplace and crinkly sheets, Veronica's ankles
propped on his shoulders. First, though, they have to find the
elusive caps, which from far away look so much like fallen fir
cones it takes a while to distinguish them from the rest of the
debris. He knows he's brought them to the same spot he found
last year, a few hundred yards north of the gravel road where
he's left the car, but now he can't be sure which hemlock trunk
was the magic one. All he remembers is a tangle of exposed
roots forming a little cave, and within it five small stalagmites
with pitted tops.

"It might help to just sit in one spot for a minute," he says.
"Let our eyes adjust."

She doesn't listen to him, just keeps crunching charcoal and
stomping deeper into the scar. He tries to follow his own advice
but so far sees only cones and the first leaves of bunchberry and
mayapple, which used to cover every inch of exposed ground
and may again one day. He knows this is the same week, if not
the same day, he found the mushrooms last year because he
took photos with his phone and recently checked the date. But
morels are notoriously fickle, and a slight difference in ground
temperature could set them back weeks. They may have come
too early, which means he'll have to return by himself during
the week—there's no chance he'll convince Sills to make this
trip a second time, not without some real promise of success. If
they can find just one cap, that might be enough, so he crouches
close to the ground, holds his face an inch about the surface, lets
his eyes unfocus so a mushroom might pop into view, as in the
psychedelic 3D posters he hung on his college dorm walls and
loved to stare at while stoned. But still, nothing.

"You know," he calls, "people in Europe used to burn their forests just so they could get a good morel crop."

"People in Europe are stupid."

He can't argue with her there. Those same Europeans banished or terrorized his ancestors, who wouldn't be caught dead in those forests lest they be hunted for sport. But he wants her to appreciate the preciousness of these little fungi, which, in their dried form, cost nearly as much per ounce as gold. *Just one*, he thinks, *and this won't have been a waste of time.* But after another half hour, neither of them has found a thing.

Then he spies what he's sure is his hemlock from last year. He recognizes the burn marks on the south-facing side of its trunk, and then the roots like a network of veins in a bony hand. But when he steps around the north side and finds the hollow, confirms that it is indeed his tree, he's disappointed once more. Beyond disappointed because, rather than the morels, what he sees are tiny stumps, freshly broken. Someone else found them first. And now he spots more evidence all around him: little white rings in the ground where hollow mushrooms have been snapped off. There are a few dozen of them, harvested within the last couple of days. He's filled with a sudden rage at the poacher who didn't leave a single morel for anyone else to find, though of course he, too, planned to harvest every one he came upon. He can only hope that the asshole missed something, but after another fifteen minutes, his containers are still empty. The discovery is devastating, but he doesn't want Sills to know, so he swallows anger and pain and puts on a face of stoic resolution. "We'll find them next time," he says, though she isn't close enough to hear.

Then she calls, "Dad, come check this out!"

He hurries over stumps and logs and roots, trips once,

nearly falls. She's just a little higher on the ridge, and maybe there, finally, they'll find what they've been looking for, and all this will have been worth the effort. But when he reaches her, she doesn't have any morels in hand. Maybe she's afraid to pick them before he's confirmed what they are, though he's already assured her there are no poisonous look-alikes, or at least none that aren't easily identified. But he doesn't see anything growing nearby. Instead she points at the sooty skeleton of a small animal, the size of a rabbit, though its skull is distinctly rodent shaped. All flesh and fur have burned away, and its teeth are still intact. "Marten," he says, "or maybe ermine. I'm not sure what the difference is. Probably had its burrow nearby."

"Fire wasn't so good for her."

"You want to bury it?"

"Are you kidding? I'm totally taking it home."

She's already got her backpack slung forward, and she lifts the skeleton with care and slides it in. On their way back to the car, he decides he'll order some dried morels through the mail, just an ounce, and when they arrive, he'll make the sherry cream sauce for her to try. Tonight they'll have to make do with pesto from a jar.

"I want to make a stand for it," Sills says. She's forgotten what they came here to find or no longer cares. She takes big strides across the singed ground, entirely gratified. "Keep it right next to my bed."

"I'll help you," he says, and they crash through the barren scar as quickly as they can until they're back on the road.

32. THE FUTURE

THE FOG IS SO thick she can't see the far bank a dozen yards across frothing water. She's up early and fully dressed—unusual for a Sunday, when she likes to lounge in bed reading a book until her father calls her out for breakfast. But he's still asleep, snoring on the couch where he must have drifted off after another bout of insomnia. It's well into spring but still cold in the mornings, which is the best time for her to catch newts. She finds them in small pools that gather on exposed volcanic rock, deep pockets where air bubbles formed a million years ago, or something like that, though the idea of a million years makes no sense to her, not really—it's hard enough to imagine what her life was like five years ago, before her parents bought the cabin, before they split, before she spent more than a few days a year in the woods where now she spends a quarter of her time.

By midsummer the pools will dry up and the newts will crawl off into the mossy undergrowth, but now it's the start of mating season, and almost every puddle she encounters houses a pair of them, their brown backs camouflaged against the algae-covered rocks, their orange bellies flashing a warning when she sticks her hand in to pick one up. They're sluggish in the cold, and she has no trouble getting her hand around them. She doesn't want to keep them, just loves the feel of them crawling on her hand and up her arm. She holds them for only a few seconds before easing them back into the water, and she never picks up the same one twice. She knows it must frighten them, believing she might try to eat them, though if she did, she'd die a terrible death. Her father has told her about the kind of poison the orange bellies caution against, one that will paralyze you and make you starve to death while your mind remains perfectly lucid. Still, she finds them so unbearably cute she can't help but spend these minutes holding as many as she can and then watching them wiggle their tails to dive back into the depths of their pools, their future, momentarily shaky, now secure.

The future is something she's been thinking about more than she might care for lately, because her language arts teacher has assigned the class a paper in which they're supposed to imagine their ideal adult life. It's a dumb assignment, meant to keep them busy near the end of the school year when they're otherwise thinking only about not riding the bus every morning and not writing dumb papers all day. She's only in seventh grade—for two more months—so why should she be thinking about adult life? It's enough to picture being in high school the year after next, in a building three times the size of her current school, with nearly two thousand kids roaming the halls. That's a future she might like to avoid, though by then maybe she'll no longer worry about kids asking why she comes to school with an overnight bag on Monday morning, why she can't come for a sleepover on the weekend.

When she does think about being a grown-up, she knows only that she doesn't want to be in Salem—the dullest town on the planet, she's told her mother, who says she felt the same way when she and Skye's father first moved here, though now she finds it quiet and charming, the perfect place to raise a kid. Skye thinks she'll raise a kid, if she has one, in a huge city full of tall buildings—San Francisco, maybe, or New York, both of which she's visited only once and remembers only slightly. Maybe Tokyo, which she knows only from the manga and anime her friend Sebastian obsesses over, showing her video clips on the phone he sneaks onto the playground and hides from the aides monitoring them. In her mind, Tokyo is nothing but neon signs she can't read and glass towers that block out the sky, and she can't really picture living there, but it's easier than actually imagining living anywhere but right here, at this cabin on the river, where she knows she'd go crazy with loneliness and boredom if she had to stay more than three nights a week.

Sebastian has no trouble with the assignment. He knows he wants to be an actor. He's a good one already, playing lead roles in musicals staged by the local theater camp two summers in a row. He's even been cast in a traveling production run by a company in Eugene. He's got a great singing voice, and he's most comfortable when everyone's looking at him. He's also the first kid she knows who has announced, publicly and loudly, that he's gay. He hasn't hit puberty yet, at least not visibly, and she wonders if he'll really start dating boys soon. She wishes she had a fraction of his certainty. He's suggested that maybe she's gay, too, and she's thought it over and wondered if that might be a good idea. But then she finds herself looking at his gray-blue eyes and thin lips and thinks that if she were going to kiss anyone before the school year ends, she'd want it to be him.

The future's a shithead, she thinks, and wants nothing to do with it. *Stay in the moment*, Sebastian has told her when she freaks out about being only a few months away from eighth grade, but it's easy for him to say when he knows what he wants in each moment to come. The moment for her is newts, and she wants to stay with them for as long as she can, but after holding a dozen, her hands are freezing, and the fog hasn't cleared at all, so after a few more minutes she goes back inside to get warm. Her father is awake and making a fire in the woodstove. He doesn't seem surprised to find she's been out already, as if he'd anticipated what she'd do before she even decided to do it.

"How are the newts?" he asks.

"Can't see a foot in front of yourself out there."

"It'll burn off by afternoon."

"Tons of them now," she says, tucking herself close to the fire, knees pulled up to her chin. "They've all paired off."

"Did you know they can live eighteen years?"

"You told me."

"Long as a cat."

"Verlaine'll live longer than that."

"Not if he keeps eating sick birds."

"They're just so much easier to catch."

"You'd think he'd learn after the first time. I got salmonella from a restaurant once. You think I went back there the next month?"

"Did you ever picture living in a place like this?" she asks. The question comes out before she can stop it, and it clearly surprises him. He tilts his head, a little bit like Verlaine does when he's considering whether or not to attack the string on her hoodie. "I mean, when you were a kid? Did you imagine this sort of life? Except for the divorce part."

"When I was a kid? I can hardly remember what I did yesterday."

"I'm serious."

"You're asking what kind of dreams I had when I was young? And how they all got crushed? And how disappointed I am with my life now?"

"Stop joking. Just answer the question."

"I don't know, Sills. I wanted to be a rock star. But I was too clumsy to play an instrument. Or too lazy to practice."

"Dad."

"I'm not kidding. Did I imagine living in the woods? Hell no. But I never imagined being a parent either. Not until I was one."

"No wonder you're so bad at it," she says, but can't keep a straight face and cracks a smile before she finishes.

"This is all better than whatever I pictured," he says. "Even the parts that suck."

"Have you ever been to Tokyo?" she asks.

"Only in Godzilla movies."

"Would you visit me if I lived there?"

"I'd visit you even if you lived in New Jersey," he says.

33. JEW'S EYES

HIS MOTHER WEARS A stricken smile the whole weekend, forcing it up whenever it begins to droop, so he's constantly reminded of her horror in the smear of dark red lipstick on her teeth. His father stepped straight into a spiderweb after getting out of the rental car on Friday afternoon, and now he waves an arm in front of his face wherever he walks. Over the past year, they've asked him lots of questions about the cabin and the surrounding area, trying to gauge whether he'd gone off the deep end and needed intervention. His mother also asked, as she did every time he moved to a new place, what sort of Jewish community was nearby. Their bafflement has only increased with each of his moves: first to North Carolina for college, then to Portland, then to Salem, a place they'd never heard of even if it was the state capital. Why did he want to live so far away? they always asked, and he always wondered, *Far away from what?* Wherever they lived was the center of the universe, as far as they were concerned. His father judges him silently as he shows them around the place, and his mother—never able to stay silent—asks endless, insufferable questions.

"That road is so twisty," she says. "Is it safe to drive on it at night? Aren't you afraid of hitting a deer?"

"The only place I ever hit a deer was in New Jersey," Lewis tells her. "Remember Shongum Road? Blind curves for a solid mile. And herds of deer on the road because everyone kept cutting the woods down. Here they've got plenty of room to roam."

His parents no longer have to worry about hitting deer, only armadillos and alligators and the occasional feral pig. They moved to a golf community in Juno Beach a decade ago, with a marina and access to the Intracoastal. His father spends his days fishing for grouper and sea bass with a pack of retired doctors and dentists—he was an optometrist for thirty-five years—who use GPS fish-finders and yak over CB radios as they ride the waves. His mother gets seasick on a calm lake, so she keeps herself busy with card games and volunteering on the club's cultural association, which arranges concerts and lectures and photography exhibits by club members with varying levels of talent. He has avoided going to see them since the divorce, but they insisted on flying out for a visit—to see Sills before she's a full-blown teenager, his mother said, though he suspects she's really here to convince him to move back to civilization.

What she says, over and over again, is how green everything is. "I just can't get over it," she says. "It's like being inside a painting."

She takes in the painting from the safety of the window but has no interest in stepping outside, though it's no longer drizzling, just gray. She keeps her hands gripped to the sides of a steaming cup of tea, her back to the woodstove. His father, tired from the trip, is napping in the loft. Sills is also wearing a big, false smile, one she won't be able to sustain all weekend, much less for the two days afterward, when his parents are taking her to Ashland to see a new production of *The Merchant of Venice.* "She needs culture," his mother said over the phone when making the plans. "She can't just look at trees all the time."

"You know she's only here on weekends," he said, but she ignored him.

"Don't you want to come with us?"

"I have to work," he said.

Now Sills doesn't seem to know what to do with herself. The cabin is too small for four of them, especially when his parents seem to take up so much space, even though they're tiny people, white-haired and wrinkled, his father not quite five and a half feet tall, his mother several inches shorter. "Bubby," Sills says. "Do you want to show me how to bake your scones? We got all the ingredients."

And then his mother fusses in the kitchen, searching for tools he obviously wouldn't have. "No pastry blender?" she asks. And later, "How do you survive without a basting brush?" But once she settles in, she finally lets her face relax. The faster her hands are moving, the calmer she is, and Sills, who's writing down the steps as she goes, has to tell her a couple of times to slow down so she can catch up. In the meantime, his mother talks at length about how much she and Sills's grandfather love Ashland—they haven't been for years, not since Lewis first moved to Oregon—and how the plays there are some of the best in the world. "We went to London a few years ago," she says, "and saw two shows at the National Theatre. Garbage compared to Ashland." Lewis bites the inside of his cheek to keep from responding. "This play we're going to see," his mother goes on, "I think it's Shakespeare's best one. People like *Hamlet*, but it's so gloomy. And *MacBeth*, forget it. Nothing but violence."

"The high school did *Romeo and Juliet* last year," Sills says.

"That's a good one," his mother replies. "But it's too sad for me."

"It's supposed to be," Sills says. "It's a tragedy."

"*Merchant* is about antisemitism," his mother says, beating eggs so hard they begin to foam.

"Well," Lewis says. "I guess you could say that. Maybe."

"Hath not a Jew eyes?" his mother says, closing hers.

"The better to eat you with," Lewis says.

"And it's got a happy ending."

"Not for Shylock," Lewis says. "But it does have a good cross-dressing part."

"I don't remember that," his mother says.

"In Shakespeare's time, it would have been a double cross. A man dressing as a woman dressing as a man."

"I don't know about all that," she says, and to shut the conversation down, she starts chopping nuts with his butcher knife, sending filbert shrapnel in all directions.

"When do we put on the cinnamon sugar?" Sills asks.

"Not until the end," his mother says.

Soon his father makes his way down, taking each step with his left foot and then easing the right behind it. He refuses to hold the railing. He's nearly eighty and needs a hip replaced. Lewis guesses he'll break it first. "Okay," he says. "I'm ready for the fish."

Lewis has warned him several times that the walk down to the bank is rocky and full of roots, and to get to the bar is a steep descent, but once again his father just waves him off, as if he's another invisible spiderweb that needs clearing away. "If I can handle a boat in the middle of a tropical depression, I can walk fifty yards," he says.

"Don't remind me," Lewis's mother says. "That storm. I was a wreck the whole day. Waiting for a call tell me your father's at the bottom of the Atlantic."

"I was in the waterway," his father says.

"Still deep enough to drown in," his mother says.

Lewis has already decided he won't let his father wade in. The current's too strong still, and the water's too cold for him to have to jump in and save him. So they cast from the bar, his father slipping on wet stones each time he lets the fly go but managing to stay upright. He's using Lewis's rod while Lewis casts with a hand-me-down from Gerry, who prefers a spinner. His father doesn't really understand the mechanics of fly casting, jerks too hard in each direction, and fails to land his tippet more than a few feet into the shallows. Lewis knows better than to try to give him tips—his father has never been one to see any value in the flipping of conventional roles. Once the father, always the father. He's not the imperious type, just firm and precise in his decisions, and generally inflexible. If Lewis is anything like him, he suspects it's only in his tendency to mope in silence whenever he's in pain.

"You know," his father says, casting badly and quickly reeling in. "If you need a loan. To get back on your feet."

"I'm on my feet," Lewis says. He takes his time with his own cast, knows he's trying to prove something with it, and lands it perfectly in an eddy just at the edge of a deep pool. "And they're exactly where I want them to be."

"Your mother worries about you," his father says.

"Not you?"

"I know you can look out for yourself. If you want to."

"Aside from my marriage being a failure," Lewis says. "And having the most tedious job on the planet. And a kid who scowls at me most of the time. I think I'm doing okay. Considering."

"She's clearly devoted to you," his father says. "For now."

"What's that supposed to mean?"

"When your sister hit fifteen," he says, "I tried to keep her close. Hung on too hard. It was a mistake. I should have let her be."

Lewis tries to remember his sister Linda at fifteen. He would have been twelve then. All he can picture is her closed bedroom door with music he hated blasting behind it, his mother in the hallway occasionally pounding or shouting through it. In these flashes, his father is nowhere near—either working late or playing tennis or sipping his evening brandy in his home office and skimming the *Times*.

Lewis says, "I'm not hanging on—"

Before he can finish, a look crosses his father's face, slightly aggrieved, an eyelid drooping, one side of his mouth going stiff. For a second Lewis thinks he's having a stroke. But then he sees: the tip of his rod has bowed. Strike, not stroke. His father still doesn't know how to work the fly rod, but he's a natural when it comes to landing a fish. He lets it run until he can get good leverage, then arches his back, pulls it ashore. It's a little rainbow, about seven inches, beautifully spotted.

His father holds up the trout, not smiling—*This is serious business*, he's always said, about most things—and Lewis snaps a picture with his phone. Then he tells him to put it back.

"This is dinner," his father says.

"It's under the size limit. Needs to be eight inches."

"This is eight. Eight and a half, easy."

"We're not using the metric system."

His father lifts the trout high and brings its head down hard on a rock. Its tail flaps once and goes still. "No point releasing a dead fish," he says. "Especially not a tasty one like this."

"Small dinner for four people," Lewis says.

"An hors d'oeuvre, then," his father says. "Unless you catch more. But that's enough for me. I need a sit."

"I only keep them when they're legal size," Lewis says.

"You're the expert," his father says and starts to climb back up the bank. Lewis, furious, is determined not to help him. He whips Gerry's rod back and forth, lets go too soon. The fly drops at his feet. From above comes a grunt, then a thud. He scrambles up to find his father sprawled on the mossy rocks, his foot still caught on a root as thick as an extension cord. "Get me up before she sees," his father whispers. "She'll never let me out of the house." Lewis takes his hand, maneuvers him gently to his knees, then lifts him to his feet. He's surprisingly light despite his round belly, as if his bones have turned hollow, like a bird's. His arm is scraped and seeping just above the wrist. "It's nothing," his father says. "Skin's gone a little thin. The wind blows and I bleed." Then he glances down and gets that aggrieved look again. "Ah, hell."

Only now does Lewis worry about his fly rod, which cost him too much to replace. He can make do with Gerry's, he tells himself, but the onrush of grief is too familiar to deny. The rod, however, looks intact. His father's expression is one reserved for fish. He landed on the little trout, which is now squashed and muddy, not much of an appetizer, much less dinner.

"I'll toss it back," Lewis says. "Otherwise we'll get scavengers."

His father brushes off his front, covers his bloody arm with a jacket sleeve. "Just pay close attention," he says. "Keep your eyes open. When she's ready to pull away, you hug her tight and then let her go."

34. EGGS

HOW LONG HAS THE rock been here? Years, at least. Probably decades. Maybe centuries. She's heard her father talk about the enormous floods that filled the valley fifteen thousand years ago, the boulders they deposited as far south as Eugene, rocks that weighed more than a car and traveled a thousand miles. This one isn't so big, flat on one side, rounded on the other, the size of a manhole cover cut in half. Its surface is pocked, volcanic, so it likely didn't come from Montana but rather from the mountains rising to the east of the cabin, obscured by clouds that drifted into the foothills in the late fall and stuck there. One of those clouds surrounds them now, leaving tiny droplets on blades of scrub grass and on the fine hairs of her arm. It's dense enough that she sometimes loses sight of the car in the driveway not a hundred yards away, and even the roof of the cabin, which is closer. Her father comes in and out of view, pushing the wheelbarrow to the mulch pile and back.

They're clearing a spot for a new garden bed. She's the one

who asked for it, because she wants to plant potatoes later this spring. *Why potatoes?* her father asked, and she didn't come up with a reason, except to say she was part Irish, wasn't she? *One tenth at most,* he said. But that plus half-Jewish, a smattering of Russian and Polish, and sure, it made sense she liked some spuds. And he agreed, nothing tasted better than home-grown. They'd live on bangers and mash next fall.

The truth is she got the idea last week when Garrick, their neighbor—her and her mother's neighbor in Salem—brought them potatoes he grew over the summer and stored in the root cellar he'd rigged up in his basement. But she doesn't want to mention Garrick to her father, doesn't want to tell him that her mother invited Garrick inside while she boiled the potatoes and cooked them into a Spanish tortilla, a dish she said she hadn't eaten for years, one she forgot she still knew how to cook. The dreaminess in her mother's voice unnerved Skye, made her say, before she could stop herself, "Did you and Dad used to eat it?" which in turn made her mother frown.

Garrick isn't terribly good-looking. Skye doesn't think so, at least. He's mostly bald, for one, and he has a little gray beard, and his face is too round, and he has a serious gut. But he's funny, that she'll admit, and she can't help enjoying the way he makes her mother laugh whenever he stops by. He's taken to calling their street "Heartbreak Alley." He got divorced a year before her parents and bought himself a metallic-blue Mini Cooper, which he calls "the midlife-crisis-mobile." He looks ridiculous driving around in it, a clown on his way to the circus, where all his chunky, middle-aged friends will climb out, gripping sore knees and stretching crimped necks.

She can't bring herself to ask whether her mother likes him, and of course if she does, her mother would deflect, saying something along the lines of "I like all our neighbors," and leave Skye to judge whether or not there was a tremble in her voice as she said it or a flush in her cheeks. So instead she asked—several hours after Garrick ate three helpings of tortilla, exclaimed over her mother's cooking, and left with a pat on each of their backs—whether her mother thought she'd ever get married again.

"God, I hope not," her mother said.

"I'm serious."

"You don't think I am?"

"It wasn't that bad."

"I think I'll be fine on my own for a while."

"For a while. That doesn't mean never."

"I suppose not."

"You don't want to have more kids, though, do you?"

"It's a little late for that."

"But you could, right? You still get your period."

"Unfortunately."

"Are you on the pill?"

"Where's all this coming from?" her mother said with a lighthearted laugh that made Skye even more uneasy. She hadn't thought until now about how her mother spent her weekends on her own, whether Garrick with his little beard and big appetite ever visited when Skye wasn't around to keep an eye on him.

"Never mind," she said.

But now, in the yard with her father, as she struggles to pry the big, flat rock from the ground where it has rested for so long, she asks, "Why'd you and Mom have only one kid?"

She's heard answers to this question before, which have changed depending on who's offering them and when: her parents were already in their mid-thirties when she was born; her mother had had two miscarriages before carrying her to term; neither of them was sure they could afford more than one child without serious compromise to their lifestyle; plus she wasn't the easiest baby, and by the time she stopped keeping them up all night, they were too exhausted to consider a second.

But now her father says, "Your mom probably would have been game for another if I'd been enthusiastic about it. But I've always been better one-on-one. I always thought a second kid would get shortchanged. Or else you would."

They finally free the rock and flip it. To its underside clings a cluster of eggs, small and white and round, the size and shape of the coriander seeds her mother grinds in a mortar and pestle and puts in soup, only wet and translucent. The sight of them turns her stomach. Her father moves to brush them off, but she stops his hand. "Wait a second," she says.

"They're slug eggs," he says. "We let them grow, your taters are history as soon as they sprout."

"Let's put it back," she says. "I don't want a dumb garden."

"We've almost got it ready."

When she insists, he gives her a look she recognizes, lips pulled to one side, hands raised in surrender—a look her mother often drew out of him—and helps her ease the rock into its hole.

"I hate potatoes," she says.

35. FREEDOM

ONE SUNDAY MORNING, A trio of ATVs tear up and down the gravel road in front of the cabin, kicking up small stones and clumps of mud, spewing clouds of ashy exhaust, and filling the canyon with relentless racket. Sills is trying to study for an algebra test, but even with headphones on, she pauses every ten minutes and shouts at the windows, and then gives Lewis a desperate, pleading look. "Can you please make them shut up?"

"It's public land," he says.

"Which means they can drive the public crazy?"

"That's what the law says."

"The law's stupid."

"God bless America."

"We should change it," she shouts as the noise draws close again, the grind and roar of oversized, unmuffled engines rattling the front windows.

"I'll call our state representative tomorrow. I'm sure he'll get right on it."

The next time the ATVs pass, Lewis steps outside to catch a glimpse of them, and the men astride the insipid vehicles look as he expects—stiff caps, camo vests, thick arms, and big bellies. Survivalist types, or rather survivalist cosplayers, the kind who fly Don't Tread on Me flags from the backs of expensive, imported pickup trucks. He's seen plenty of them in his year living up here, has shared a table with some in the highway tavern and listened to them spout off about the evils of the government without letting on that he works for the state, and he's come to think of them as mostly harmless, at least individually. They join groups like the Three Percenters so they can drink beer together and shoot up targets in old clear-cuts. But he's also seen plenty in Salem in his decade working near the capitol—protesting carbon cap bills, mining restrictions, ranching regulations, timber protections—has watched them march through downtown fully armed, assault rifles slung over their backs, pistols in holsters at their sides, all somehow legal (i.e., "the law's stupid"), so he also doubts his assessment of them as harmless, especially when they're together in groups.

And when they're in their element, expressing their freedom to menace others with noisy, powerful machines, he guesses their potential for harm reaches its pinnacle, especially were he to try to get in their way. They glare at him as they pass, the closest swerving off the road's shoulder to flatten one of the ferns at the edge of his property. They might be in their twenties or in their forties—it's hard to tell with their scruffy facial hair, cap brims shading their features, mud splattered on their arms. One of them comes close enough for Lewis to see a tattoo not yet covered in grime, of an eagle carrying an anchor in one talon, a skull in the other. The wheels of the ATV are wider than those on his car. They've gouged deep rivets in the road that likely won't get repaired for years; working for the DOT, he knows how little budget there is for any projects that aren't essential—crumbling bridges, overpasses, highways— and rural roads are the last to get any attention.

He's relieved when they ride higher up the ridge, onto Forest Service land, though their motors still buzz and echo over the river. While they're gone, he takes the opportunity to move some rocks from the ground near his side of the fence to line the edge of the road. Some are big around as basketballs, others pointed and jagged. "Let's see if I interfered with their freedom," he says to Sills when he goes back inside. She's given up on algebra and is instead painting small stones—a project she invented for herself during the darkest days of winter— which she distributes around the backyard. Some look like ladybugs, others turtles. Now she's turning a long, narrow one into a woolly bear caterpillar.

"I bet they'll ride right over them," she says.

"They're free to blow their tires all they want."

But when he hears them tearing back down the hill, he can't bring himself to go outside and watch. Around these types of men, he feels strangely on display. He sees himself through their eyes as a caricature—his hair darker and curlier, his nose longer and bumpier, his hands grabbing stacks of coins. An image straight out of *The Protocols of the Elders of Zion*. He normally gives his Jewishness little thought or space in his conception of himself but feels it most acutely in moments of vulnerability. He's sure if the ATV riders knew what he was, that's all they'd see. So he stays inside, peering around the edge of the window as the vehicles come into view, waiting to see how they'll navigate his new obstacles. Directly in front of the cabin is the flattest and widest part of the road, and they use it to spin donuts, but this time instead of skimming his yard, one of them cuts right across it, skirting the new rocks and leaving muddy gashes on either side of the front walkway.

And then Sills is out the front door, shouting and waving her arms. The ATVs have stopped in front of her, two angled uphill, one aimed directly at her knees. If he hesitates, it's only for a moment. Of that, he's sure. He's already telling himself as he rushes across the room that he hasn't left his daughter to face these men alone, that he acted as soon as he realized what was happening. But by the time he makes it outside, it's over. The ATVs are speeding off down the hill and soon disappear around the bend. Blocked by the big, moss-draped maples below, their engines fade to a distant puttering. Sills crouches to tend a mangled patch of salal. One broken branch, she twists off and tosses to the side.

"Assholes," she says.

"What did you say to them?"

"That my dad was getting his shotgun, and they better get out of here quick."

"You didn't."

"I just told them to get off our yard."

"That's it?"

"They apologized. But they're still assholes."

"Guys like that," he says and finds himself shaking, "they can be dangerous. You don't really want to mess around."

"They get big motors to make up for little dicks. That's what Mom says."

"Next time let me handle it."

She shrugs, moves some dirt over the salal's exposed roots. A strand of fine, sandy hair falls in front of her face, and she brushes it behind an ear, leaving a streak of mud on her temple.

He's glad he hasn't burdened her with anxiety the way his parents did him, hasn't made her believe there's treachery waiting for her in the world just because of who she is, that she'd best stay close to home. Maybe there's freedom in it. Or maybe he's left her exposed to what's really out there. As with most parenting choices, he doesn't know which is worse.

36. TRAMP

SHE'S SPENT MOST OF the night in one corner of the gym, in a tight clump of her friends. Sometimes they step out onto the floor to hop around together; a few other times they've all gone to the bathroom to look themselves over in the mirror. Skye is wearing what she wore to school that day: a nicer shirt than usual, light blue and long-sleeved with a wide neckline, and her usual jeans. She hasn't had a chance to go home to change. It's a Friday night, and normally she'd be at the river by now, but after ballet her father took her out for tacos and dropped her back off at school for the mixer. All her friends have dressed up: Kendall in a short skirt that makes her look chubbier than usual, Lizzy elegant in a dress to her knees, June in tuxedo pants and a men's white button-down with the sleeves cut off. They let Skye borrow makeup, and she smudges her eyelids until they're a dark, dusky purple that makes her look either sultry or sleepy. She can smell her sweat from ballet practice, which is soon covered by fresh sweat as she dances with the girls.

Most of the boys in her grade stay on the opposite side of

the gym, playing a game with a little rubber ball which occasionally bounces over their heads, so they have to chase it down in the middle of the dance floor, where they flail their arms for a minute, out of rhythm with the music, before heading back to their side. There are only a few people who dance to the slow songs—the two gay and proudly out couples everyone envies for their confidence and self-possession, including Sebastian and his new boyfriend, as well as their old friend Aliyah with her date, Trayton Bush. Aliyah no longer hangs out with their group, either because she thinks she's too good for them or because they've alienated her by mocking her horsey laugh. Skye wavers between feeling justified and feeling guilty whenever she sees Aliyah sitting with Trayton at lunch. She no longer has a crush on Trayton, or at least no longer wants to—he's funny and cute enough, but all he talks about is baseball—and now she tries not to watch him with his hands on Aliyah's hips, swaying idiotically as she pulls him closer and wraps her arms around his neck.

Only toward the end of the night do some of the other boys—a few in dress shirts and khakis, most in T-shirts, any who started with ties now wearing them around their foreheads—nudge each other to approach. The first walks up to Lizzy, which is no surprise; the second, Kendall. Skye turns to June and suggests they go visit the bathroom. She wants to avoid the embarrassment of standing there alone. She wishes she were gay, wishes she wanted to dance with June, who'd let her put her chin on her shoulder the way Aliyah does with Trayton.

But before she can start to walk away, there's a tap on her elbow. A boy she's never once spoken to looks down at his feet and asks if she wants to dance. He's been in her algebra class all year, and she knows his name is Andrew, but she's never taken much notice of him before. He's small and dark, with thick, black hair and very white teeth. At least one of his parents is Indian, she thinks, though his last name is Johnson. Now he's standing a few inches from her with his hands cupping her waist. She reaches across the space between them and lets her own hands drop onto his shoulders, which are narrow and bony. He flinches at her touch and quickly starts to turn a circle, too fast for the song's listless tempo. He mostly keeps his gaze focused on the floor, at her feet in the running shoes she always wears with ankle socks to keep them from stinking. When he glances up, she tries to smile at him, but her face feels funny doing so, and he quickly looks away. They don't say anything as they turn. She doesn't know if she likes the pressure of his hands on her waist, but she doesn't think she dislikes it. When they pass close, Aliyah gives her a little wave over Trayton's shoulder.

Andrew takes deep breaths—concentrating, it seems, or maybe counting down until the song is over. It's a dumb song anyway, about a breakup and someone driving around afterward, looking at restaurants and movie theaters and other places guaranteed to make her sad. When it comes to a close, she immediately feels Andrew's hands beginning to leave her sides. She's not ready for that yet, or else she thinks Aliyah might still be watching and will come away with the idea Skye fears most: that she's still a little kid, not ready for a close dance or a date or a boyfriend or the things other girls their age seem to want. She doesn't know if she wants any of those things, doesn't think she wants a boyfriend, and certainly not if it were Andrew, who doesn't say anything or look at her when the song ends. But before he can walk away, she clamps down on his shoulders to keep him from moving. And then she steps forward, not to give him a hug, exactly, just a press of her body against his, to see how it feels, which is strange and dizzying, especially because he does look up at her then, dark eyes wide and startled, maybe terrified, her chest against his, bellies touching through shirts, thighs through jeans. She holds him there for just a moment and then lets him go, and he hurries off to the gaggle of boys and their rubber ball.

If any of her friends notice, none says a word. June comes back from the bathroom, yawns dramatically, says she's never been so bored in her life. Lizzy complains about no one knowing how to ballroom dance or salsa; she's the only one in the whole school who's ever taken lessons. Kendall looks as if she's about to cry, but when Skye asks what's wrong, she just shrugs and shakes her head. After two more songs the mixer is over. She doesn't see Andrew again when they leave. Her father's car is in the same place in the parking lot as when he dropped her off, and only when she reaches it does she realize he's been here the whole time, dozing, because of course it's too far for him to drive home and back and he has nowhere else to go. He's startled when she opens the door, gives her that disgruntled look he often turns on her when he wakes from too long a nap. "What's with your eyes?" he says. "Did you rub charcoal on them?"

When they get to the cabin, she tries to wash the makeup off, but she doesn't have any of her mother's witch hazel wipes here, nothing but hand or dish soap, neither of which completely remove the smudges. All weekend a faded gray lingers on her eyelids, which she forgets about until she catches herself in the mirror, and then she goes at them again with soap. She could ask her father to take her to the store, but she doesn't want to bother. After a while she decides she likes the look of it, the shade of fading bruises. She looks older, harder, more experienced. The smudges are still there Monday morning when she's back at school. They make her look as if she's never gone home, never left the gym. In algebra class June says, "Hey, tramp. Looking good."

Across the room, Andrew keeps his head down, furiously solving for x.

37. TWO TRUNKS

THERE'S A TREE AT the southeast corner of the property, just before it dips toward the riverbank, that has always bugged him. It's old and healthy, with a trunk that forks about twelve feet off the ground. What bothers him is that it was once two trees growing close together for decades, before their trunks touched and then merged as they continued their push upward, sharing bark and roots and whatever energy the needles synthesize high overhead. They are no longer distinguishable as two separate beings, can no longer live apart. They have fused into one, even unto death.

Yes, it's now a year since the final definitive split, the signing of documents, and he's feeling particularly down. He would have found the tree an absurd metaphor for marriage while he was still in it, but now he feels as if he's been pulled up by the roots and torn in half, a huge swath of him left exposed to pests and rot. Would he and Veronica have been better off if they'd maintained a little space between them, if they hadn't gone all in? Would the rift feel any less painful?

He spends the morning sitting on a stump with his coffee, brooding over the tree and wondering whether he can bring himself to cut it down. True, it provides morning shade and privacy from the neighbors, habitat for birds and squirrels, but it tortures him all the same. He can't afford to hire a tree service to take it out, and he's never used a chainsaw, even though Gerry has offered to lend him one any time he needs it. He's always imagined the blade springing backward and cutting off a foot or gouging his jugular. Maybe a windstorm will split the trunks. He could live with one of them left standing on its own, though the one most likely to fall, given its curve, would take out the deck. Maybe it's best to have something to stare at with hatred, a repository for all his resentment.

Sills finds him there, after how long he doesn't know. His back hurts from hunching forward with elbows on knees. His coffee is cold. "You left the fridge open," she says.

"Did I?"

"Not like there's much in there to spoil."

"I'll drop by the store later."

"There's bread. And a box of spaghetti. We'll be okay for the day." The stump is narrow, but she wedges herself beside him, her arm pressing against his. He scoots over an inch, and she scoots closer. He can't bring himself to look at her. If he does, she's sure to see what's on his mind.

"Do you think that tree could hit the house if it splits?" he asks.

"People afraid of trees falling on them shouldn't move to the woods," she says. "That's what you told me."

"Sounds pretty wise," he says. "Until a tree falls on you."

"Are you going to stare at it all day?"

"You have something better in mind?"

"We could go see a movie."

"Long drive."

"I'm used to it."

"Anything good playing?"

"Does it matter?"

"I guess not."

"Even a bad movie's better than doing nothing."

"I wasn't doing nothing. I was waiting for the tree to fall on me."

"A watched tree never falls," she says.

"You're full of wisdom today."

"You know," she says, and her voice has a bit of a tremble in it, enough to make him turn to face her. Even under heavy clouds, her eyes shine with moisture. "You could start dating again. It's been long enough. I mean, I'd be okay with it. If you wanted. As long as you don't tell me about it. Or make me meet any of them. Or start swiping your phone all the time. That would be creepy." She stands then and walks quickly toward the cabin. "Forget I said it. I don't want to know. Let's go see a crappy movie."

38. HOWL

WHEN HER EYES OPEN, she can see only her father's silhouette against the shaded window. He shakes her shoulder again, whispers, "Time to get up now. Quickly." For a second she thinks it must be Monday morning and she must have slept through her alarm, but it's June and school just ended for the year, and her theater camp hasn't yet begun, so there's no reason for her to get up early. And even if there was, wouldn't it be lighter than this? As she sits up, she catches sight of the clock, the glowing teal numbers reading 1:42.

"What's going on? Why'd you get me up in the middle of the night?"

"You'll see. Come on."

She starts to look for clothes, but he tells her to forget it, to just throw on a jacket and shoes; it's warm enough out, and they won't be too long. She's wearing pajamas that would embarrass her if anyone saw them—matching shorts and tank top printed with cartoon bunnies—but who's going to see her at two in the morning in the middle of nowhere? She does what he says, and though she's still groggy and disoriented, curiosity makes her follow him out the front door and up the path to the road. He's hurrying ahead, far enough that she loses sight of him for a second, only hears the crunch of his feet on gravel, and then his whisper again: "Come on. Quickly."

Then her eyes adjust to the light, and she sees him up ahead, where the road takes a curve past Gerry's house and flattens out in a clearing. And it's lighter than she first realized because the moon is full, and the sky is mostly free of clouds, though a few puffy ones drift across the open space between treetops. When she catches up to him, her father waves his hands, cupped together over his head, as if to blow the clouds away. "Go," he says. "Damn it, go."

And they seem to obey, floating to the east and leaving the moon alone in the wide space between the tips of firs that hold it in a jagged container. Her father glances at his phone and counts down. "Thirty, twenty-nine, twenty-eight—wait a minute. Let's lie down for this."

"In the middle of the road?"

"We'll hear if anyone's coming."

She's down before he is, listening to him groan as he lowers himself and sigh when he's on his back. Sharp bits of gravel press into her shoulder blades and butt. "What are we doing?" she asks, but now it doesn't really matter. She's glad to be doing something weird at two in the morning in the middle of the woods. It's better than being asleep and missing out on everything, as she often believed when she was younger—all the exciting, adult things happening without her while she suffered confusing dreams.

He's counting down again. "Ten, nine, eight."

The anticipation is too much for her not to ask, "Is this like the end of the world or something? A nuclear bomb about to fall on us?"

But he keeps going: "Four, three, two—keep looking up there!"

And soon she sees: a small nibble taken out of the left side of the moon. "Is this what I think it is?" she asks.

"The full deal," her father says.

"How come you didn't tell me it was coming?"

"Didn't want to get your hopes up. In case it was cloudy. Still likely enough this time of year."

The nibble has become a bite. Her father passes her a pair of binoculars, and through it she can see a dark line against the chalky gray surface. Where it has already passed is now a faint, dusky orange. "Is that really our shadow?"

"In ancient China they believed it was a dragon swallowing the moon whole."

"And then what, it would poop it back out?"

"The Incans thought it was a jaguar. And after it finished with the moon, it would come eat all the animals on earth. So they'd dance around with spears and shout at the moon to hold it back."

"How do you know all this crap?"

"Wikipedia. I read it this morning."

"My history teacher says it's not a credible source."

"Don't hog the binocs," he says.

She passes them back. The dark line is approaching the big, dark crater close to the moon's center. The slow movement of it makes her feel smaller and smaller, as if she's receding into the distance. When there's still a sliver of brightness remaining, she lets out a howl, her best imitation of a coyote. She's heard them up here from time to time, though not since last summer.

It makes her feel slightly more present, though still drifting on a rock in space, tethered only to the disappearing moon. Her father howls too. And then they hear a howl in response, maybe a quarter mile downstream. They aren't the only people out watching the world go dark, the entire disk above them now the orange of old rust. Another howl sounds farther in the distance, and then one closer, and she and her father are both howling now, a big chorus of howls. Maybe there's even an actual coyote's voice in the mix, though more likely it's someone's dog. The canyon is alive with the sound, and if there were anything scary about the dark woods surrounding them, all terror has been chased away by the force of air passing through their lungs. She howls until she's out of breath, then sucks in and lets loose again. The moon is still covered. She doesn't know if she wants it to stay that way or for the light to return.

"How long does it last?" she asks.

"About an hour," her father says. "Could be longer."

"Can we stay?"

"Long as you want."

She howls again, but this time it feels a little forced. She doubts she can keep it up for an hour. Before she can try again, another voice calls in the darkness, "What the hell's going on out here? It's the middle of the goddamn night!"

"Gerry," her father whispers.

"People are trying to sleep!" Gerry cries.

Skye snickers. Her father does too. Once they start, they can't stop. She lets out another cackling howl.

"Shut the hell up already!" Gerry yells, which only makes them laugh harder.

"Do you think he has a gun?" she asks when she catches her breath.

"Let's not find out," her father says, but she howls again

anyway. She can't help it. They roll over, push themselves up, creep as quietly as they can around the bend. The light above Gerry's front door is on, blaringly bright, and after she glances at it, she can't see anything else—it follows her, flashing against her retina, blinding her to everything. If Gerry is out there, pacing in front of the house with a rifle, she can't spot him. They make it past without trouble and reach the cabin, but now the moon is blocked by trees. She can't tell if it's starting to emerge from the shadow. She's glad not to know.

"Next one's in three years," her father says. "And in February. Chances it'll be clear then are pretty slim. So better get all your howling out now."

Three years from now is impossible to imagine. How anyone can see so far ahead—to know what the moon will do then, to know anything that might happen—baffles her. Maybe she doesn't believe it. There's no point in saving her breath, in any case. She pulls it into her lungs, tilts her head back, and lets everything out.

39. FATHER'S DAY

THEY PASS A STUFFED black bear clinging to the trunk of a Douglas fir and then float into a long wooden shed, inside of which animatronic mill workers feed a log to a spinning buzzsaw. Lewis is inside another log, this one lined with plastic cushions, and Sills reclines on him as they bob down a fiberglass stream.

Most of her friends have spent weekends at Disneyland, but this is all he can afford: a day at the Enchanted Forest, a tiny amusement park just south of Salem and built in the 1970s by a lunatic who loved kids and European fairy tales. It's full of creepy mechanized dolls: the witch wagging a finger at Gretel while Hansel warns her from a cage, Pinocchio coming alive with the touch of a fairy's wand, blackbirds sprouting from a pie to sing a song of sixpence. He finds their own forest more enchanting, but the place brings out something in Sills, a child-ish glee he almost never sees anymore, so he doesn't mind standing in long lines or trudging up and down hilly paved paths in the sudden heat of late June. There are only so many more days when she'll grab his hand and pull him along like this, with a wild smile and flashing eyes. He's always been irritated by parents who say they wish their kids would stay young forever—isn't the whole point of parenting to help them grow into adults?—but right now he might like to freeze time just briefly, take a little pause and hold things right where they are, in this fake log in a fake stream, her back against his chest, a little squeal emerging as a cable pulls them up toward the first small plunge.

This is their last ride of the day, the one Sills has been saving until just before they leave. He's survived the little roller coaster meant to look like a bobsled, which takes sharp curves on its side and always seems as if it's just about to topple off its rickety ice mountain, as well as the haunted house with its sinister music and ghouls that spring out at you on hidden tracks. He scored high on the Challenge of Mondor, a target-shooting game in a cave of dragons and trolls—he earned knight level to Sills's knight-in-training, but since when did knights fight monsters with infrared guns?—and she pummeled him on the bumper cars. After this, they'll get ice cream and head home.

But first he has to make it through the log ride, which begins pleasantly enough, a calm meander through the trees, until suddenly the bottom drops out of the stream, the log jolts down while his stomach and balls ascend, and Sills screams in his ear. She talked him out of donning one of the plastic ponchos the ride operator handed out at the loading dock, and now water splashes onto his bare knees, chilling him even when they take the next turn and leave the shade of a maple, the sun flashing on the water ahead momentarily blinding him as they take the second small dip.

Then they're climbing again, toward the big drop he eyed closely when they entered the ride, thinking it wasn't really so high or so steep, though now as the log crests the top, it's far higher than anything he could have imagined, and angled straight down. How can he let his child fling herself from this cliff? His own parents never went on rides with him, leaving that to his older sister. He'd grown up going to a treacherous New Jersey water park notorious for accidents and lawsuits— twice he'd almost drowned in its wave pool—and now he can't imagine how his parents would have allowed it.

"Oh my God oh my God oh my God," Sills chants as they edge toward the peak and tip forward. *I've killed us*, he thinks. Below them are dozens of other dads with their kids, waiting to take their turn. *We've killed them all*, he tells himself as the log drops and the wind hits his face and Sills's scream bursts his brain, and then buckets of water wash over his face and down his chest, and he must let out a noise that Sills finds hilarious, because she's cracking up now, those wild eyes turning to taunt him—"I'm hardly wet at all!"—and the smile he'd pay to see instead of the glower she turns on him whenever she knows he's looking, or worse, the sorrowful expression he catches when she isn't aware he's in the room. His heart is pounding, and his hands are cramped on the rails of the fake log, and since he didn't die, he supposes he feels more alive than ever.

"That was amazing," Sills says. "Can we do it again?"

"We're out of tickets."

"You could buy more, couldn't you?"

"You really want your old man to die of a heart attack before he's fifty?" Lewis asks as they bob around one last turn toward the exit.

"I do," she says. "I totally do."

SUMMER

40. LOST

LATE ONE NIGHT SHE wakes to the sound of screaming and remembers once more that her family has fallen apart. In the dark, rising out of dreams, she believes she's still in Salem, in her bedroom facing a streetlamp only partially blocked by the leaves of an old oak. And her parents are downstairs in the living room or kitchen, yelling at each other, though their words are indistinguishable, her mother's high-pitched, her father's garbled by growls. They never fought this way when they were still married. They'd just exchange angry whispers or sit in silence, her mother fuming, her father pretending nothing was wrong. Skye often wished they'd just shout or throw things and get it over with. Why are they doing so now, when it's already too late, when her father has moved out for good?

The screams draw closer, louder. But they no longer sound as if they're coming from two different people. Just her mother, then, venting all her frustration to the empty house. Or has someone broken in to rob and murder them? She's all the way awake now, and the window begins to take shape, not the narrow one with wooden slats crossing the panes, framed by lavender curtains, but a stretch of glass as wide as her bed. The light isn't from the streetlamp but the moon, half-full, hazy behind thinning clouds and evergreen needles. Not in Salem, then. So not her mother screaming. Her father?

When she gets out of bed and leaves her room, she finds him sitting quietly in the dark, stretched out on the couch beside the tall window that faces the river. He's dressed in shorts and a T-shirt, his hair mussed in its usual way, his jaw dark with stubble. She can't tell if he's also been roused by the noise or if he'd already been up. How could she have imagined the screams coming from him? They're terrified and helpless but not human. No one she knows could sound this way. But she doesn't want to know what can, not yet.

"What time is it?" she asks instead.

"Don't know," her father says. "Late."

"You've been up?"

"I might have dozed a bit."

"You should quit drinking caffeine," she says. "Mom started taking melatonin."

He gestures at the window, through which she can spy tree trunks splitting a bright spot of river reflecting a broken moon. "Don't you want to see?"

"I guess."

"Right there. It keeps running from the driveway to the deck and back."

He doesn't make room for her, so she kneels on the opposite end of the couch, just past his bare feet. At first she can't make out anything. But when the screams—*No*, she thinks, *shrieks*—come close again, she catches a flash of movement, a dark shape against the dark ground. On the next pass she sees it more clearly, a furry thing the size of a dinner plate with a tail trailing on the ground. It runs to the far side of the driveway, stops and shrieks behind the car, and then runs back. Its frantic darting somehow makes the sound more agonized. She wants her father to make it stop, but he only gazes out placidly, hands behind his head, eyes sleepy and content.

"What is it?" she asks.

"Can't you see?"

"That sound is horrible."

"It's just scared. It'll be okay."

"What is it?" she asks again. But this time the creature passes through a stretch of moonlight, and when it comes close, she can make out the stripes on its tail, the pointed nose, the dark mask around the eyes. "Raccoon," she says. "Baby?"

"Got separated from the rest of the family," her father says. "I saw them earlier in the week. Mom and three little ones."

"We should help it," she says.

"It'll run off if we go out there. Then it might really get lost."

"I wish it would stop making that noise."

"I used to say the same thing when you were an infant. Screaming your lungs out every time we put you in the car seat."

The little raccoon runs across the yard again, but it's slower now, getting tired. This time, after it shrieks, it stays still at the edge of the driveway, hunched low, face tucked down between its paws. "Can't we do anything?" she asks.

"Being scared isn't always a bad thing," he says.

"Try telling that to the raccoon."

"And anyway, it seems scarier than it really is. Look. It's already getting used to the idea of being on its own."

It shrieks again but stays where it is.

"Why isn't its mom coming?"

"She will."

In the woods, nothing moves. The baby raccoon lies there, silent and lost.

"Where the hell is she?" Skye whispers. She kicks her father's foot.

"She'll come," he says, with confidence that only makes her doubt him more. "She'll be here soon."

41. FREAKY

WORD HAS SLOWLY SPREAD among his old Portland friends, though often the details get distorted in the passage from one to another. "Hey man, I hear you're living off the grid," one says on his cell phone's voice mail. "Good for you. I looked into solar for my place, but too many trees in the neighborhood to make it efficient."

In his decade in Salem, none of these friends ever visited, though at first he often invited them to come down and see his new place some weekend, bring the kids and barbecue. They'd say they wanted to but had to practice with their softball team or take the kids to visit their cousins, but maybe they'd stop by for lunch one day on their way to the beach, if they took the long route and if the kids didn't fall asleep on the way; or maybe they'd come down and camp in his backyard, as if it weren't only an hour away and Lewis didn't make the drive up regularly to meet them for a beer after work.

Now he gets three calls in a month from people saying

they want to check out the cabin; their kids could finally meet, they'd get along for sure, and they could all go fishing or hiking or whatever the fuck it was he did in the woods all year. Davo is the most insistent and convincing—"I really miss you, man, it's been way too long since we've caught up"—and the one who seems least likely to interrupt his time with Sills. He and Davo worked together at a downtown Portland hotel when Lewis first moved there—still disoriented after his four years of college in North Carolina, where he lost his New Jersey accent, his virginity, and his ambitions to be a journalist—Davo as a server in the banqueting department, Lewis as a bartender. They didn't have much in common—they didn't like the same music, which normally would have meant Lewis wanted nothing to do with him—but their long shifts together, and the longer drinking sessions afterward, cemented a unique bond, and for a while Lewis considered him one of his closest friends.

They haven't seen each other since Davo's divorce, which finalized two years before Lewis's, and Lewis has often felt guilty for not reaching out to support him at the time. But now Davo sounds happier than he's been in years. "I got this new girl," he says when Lewis returns his call. "She's amazing. I mean, we've only been together a few weeks, but it's, like, the best thing ever, and I got this little trailer for us to camp in. You know, one of those little teardrops? Just enough room for two. We'll park it in your driveway, and you'll hardly know we're there."

And it's true. After Lewis gives them a tour of the cabin and the yard on the Friday night they arrive—late, after Sills is already asleep—they disappear into the trailer and don't emerge until nearly noon the next day. Davo looks healthier than the last time Lewis saw him—bald now, but with less of a paunch—and the new girlfriend is young and slender, though a little too haggard for Lewis to consider her attractive. Her teeth are crooked and coffee stained, her eyes bloodshot. There's a slow, dreamy quality to her speech—"I've heard *so* much about you. I'm *so* glad to finally meet you"—that suggests a permanent high. Davo has remained in the service industry—he's now managing a steakhouse only a few blocks from the hotel where they met—and it has aged him more than Lewis's decade in a cubicle, though Davo tells him Pilates has saved him. His back was worse than Lewis's a few years ago, but now that he goes to classes twice a week, he hasn't taken a single Aleve in months. He looks like he could be heading to a Pilates class now, in spandex shorts and a mesh tank top that shows off a tuft of graying hair just below his throat.

Davo exclaims over how big Sills has gotten, and Sills pretends to remember him, though she hasn't seen him since she was three or four and clearly has no idea who he is. She shows the girlfriend her room and then shows her the path down to the river, and while they're gone, Davo says, "This is a pretty sweet setup, man. Great place to get back on your feet. Clear your head for a while. Play hermit."

"I'm not playing," Lewis says. "I'm the real deal."

"But for real. When you moving back up to P-town?"

"Kid's only in middle school. I can't move away till she's in college."

"Hardly farther than this. Closer if you're in the south suburbs."

"Suburbs give me hives," Lewis says.

"Seriously, though. You can't stay here forever. You gotta get back in the game. And trust me"—Davo jerks his head toward the river, where the girlfriend, in tiny shorts that show off her bony hips, is climbing back up the bank—"it's a whole new world out there. The girls now, man, they're freaky." He draws out the last word and makes a whistling sound, though it's less an actual whistle than a high-pitched honk. Lewis takes in the freaky girlfriend, her knobby legs as skinny as Sills's, veins visible on pale thighs, blown-out pupils from whatever pills she crushes and snorts. And despite himself, he envies Davo's bliss, no matter how fleeting or illusory it might be.

"It's *so* beautiful," the girlfriend says. "Let's go for a walk, babe."

Lewis tells them how to find the trailhead along the river, but instead they just stroll up the road, holding hands, the girlfriend wearing flip-flops that keep slipping on loose stones. When they're out of sight, Sills says, "That's your . . . friend?"

"Of course. Why do you say it like that?" he asks, though he knows why and knows his defensiveness sounds hollow.

"He's just really different."

"It's good to have people in your life who aren't like you."

"His girlfriend's . . . nice?"

"And?"

"Kinda weird? She kept telling me I need a lock on my door."

Lewis doesn't notice when they come back, or else they purposely sneak around the house to keep him from watching them slip into the teardrop trailer. But he sees it shuddering in the late afternoon and again in the early evening, and he tries to feel happy for Davo, who was truly miserable when his marriage ended, though its ending had been entirely his fault, even more so than Lewis's—he'd had multiple affairs, had ridiculed his wife when she'd gained weight, had always prioritized going out with friends over parenting. And now he doesn't seem to mind that he sees his kids only a few hours a week, that his custody agreement doesn't allow them to spend the night. At his core, Lewis has always believed Davo is a good guy, though *good* might be a relative term and dependent upon proximity. Right now, at least, he seems to be good to the freaky new girl-friend at least ten years his junior, or she's good to him, or at least they're having good sex, which is more than Lewis can say for himself.

"Aren't they gonna come out for dinner?" Sills asks.

"I guess we'll see," he answers.

He's planned a special meal, roasting chicken and potatoes on the open fire drum he's built from the bottom of an old pro-pane tank he painted black to make it look like a cauldron. He waits as long as possible to get the fire going, and then waits until it's down to coals before putting the food wrapped in foil on to cook, but even when it's dark out and the food is finished, they don't appear, and he and Sills eat on the deck alone.

"I think you should get some new friends," she says.

He takes a bite but doesn't answer.

Davo finally comes out soon after Sills goes to bed. It must be close to ten. Lewis is still tending the fire, though it's warm enough without it. "Hey, man," Davo whispers and holds up his phone. "No service out here. You got a phone inside, right?"

"Sure. You need something?"

"I think I better make a call." In the flickering dimness, Lewis can't see his face, but there's concern in his voice and in the stiffness of his walk as he comes up the deck stairs.

"Everything okay?"

"I think she's probably fine. Just overdid it a little."

"Overdid?" Lewis says, louder than he means to. "Are you telling me—"

"Nah, man. She's breathing." He pauses, takes a long, trembling breath. "She just won't wake up."

"What's she on?"

"I try not to ask," Davo says, and now Lewis hears the break in his voice, the snot-filtered whimper that made Lewis avoid returning his calls during the divorce. "I really dig her, man, but she's a fuckin' mess."

"It'll take an ambulance at least forty-five minutes to get out here. Maybe an hour."

Davo shakes out his arms, rubs his face. "Okay. Okay. I guess I better haul ass back to civilization." He gives Lewis a hug and hurries to the car. Over his shoulder, he calls, "Thanks for everything, man. We still need to catch up."

And then he's pulling away, the trailer bouncing down the gravel road with a passed-out girl inside. In the morning, when Sills asks what happened to them, he says only, "They had an early appointment."

"I like your other friends better," she says.

"I think I do too."

On Monday morning, there's a text from Davo waiting on his cell phone: *All good. Woke up before we got to e room. Little banged up from the drive. And pissed off beyond belief. Fuckin spitfire. Anyway, sorry for early exit. Let's do it again soon.*

42. BLOOD

SHE CLOSES THE FRONT of the washer as quietly as she can, hoping not to wake him. But as soon as she presses the start button and water hisses through the pipes, she hears him stirring overhead. Water sprays onto the sheets from the sides and above, and the soap starts to foam, but not fast enough to wash away the bright red streak from the white cotton. Damn this place for coming with a front-loading washer with a porthole window on the front. Who needs to watch laundry spinning around? These things should happen in private, she thinks, behind opaque metal, as in the Salem house, where the washer is in the garage, freezing in winter and roasting now, which means she never wants to do her own laundry there. Having it in the closet outside her bedroom here has been one of the things she's enjoyed about the cabin, and except for the glass front, she's grateful for it now when she's been so stupid as to forget to bring tampons with her this weekend, though she knew her period could come at any time.

The truth is, this is only her fourth period ever, and they haven't yet come regularly enough to keep each from taking her by surprise. The first was eight months ago, and it started in the afternoon when she was already home from school; her mother arrived an hour later, hugged her, and cried, which embarrassed Skye as much as it comforted her. Since then, she's usually carried what she needs in her backpack, and she's never had a problem.

But somehow it's never quite occurred to her that it might happen in the cabin, that her father might be the only one around. Maybe she thought she could stay a kid forever out here in the woods, or maybe she can't bear the idea of her father recognizing the changes that have happened to her body over the last year. In either case, she shuts the closet door as his footsteps creak on the stairs.

"You're up early," he says.

"The birds woke me."

"Those jays never shut up."

"And then I spilled orange juice on my bed."

"You know you shouldn't bring food in there," he says. "The ants were bad enough this spring. We really don't want to have to deal with mice."

"I know."

Orange juice was a stupid thing to say, but she knows they have some in the fridge, so it's a lie she can back up and get away with for now. Would have been better if they had tomato juice, but she thinks it's disgusting, and her father will drink it only with hot sauce and vodka, and he's been avoiding hard alcohol—to keep his weight down, he says, though he still drinks a beer or two with dinner most nights she's here, and his little bit of extra belly hasn't changed in size. She's bunched a thick wad of toilet paper in her underwear but doesn't know how long it'll last. It's only Saturday, in any case, and she'll certainly need to get to the store before the weekend is over. The key is figuring out how to get there without telling him the reason.

"We're out of bananas," she says.

"We've got strawberries. From the farmer's market."

"I'm craving bananas."

"You'll have to make do for now."

"Can't we go into town?"

"Not before I've had some coffee."

The washer has finished filling and begun its first agitation. She opens the door a crack. The suds are pink. She feels the toilet paper sticking to the inside of her thigh. Back in the bathroom, she rinses, dabs herself clean with more paper to keep from soiling any of the towels, and makes a new wad in her underwear. In the mirror, she's pale, almost greenish, as if all the blood is draining out of her. Before she comes out, her father calls through the door, "Check the bottom drawer. Left side."

She opens it. Inside are two boxes of tampons, her mother's brand, along with a pack of pads, another of liners. Once the initial relief passes, she's more mortified than grateful. Why do bodies have to be so strange and visible and out of your control? She puts in a tampon the way her mom showed her. At least she doesn't need help with that part anymore. The wrapper she shoves to the bottom of the garbage, underneath a spent toothpaste tube and an empty package of her father's razors and a bunch of used tissues. Then she spends a solid minute washing her hands.

When she comes out, her father says, "Your mom told me to keep them on hand."

She nods, says nothing.

"You know, you don't have to keep stuff from me. I'm a grown-up. I can handle it."

She nods again.

"You still want to go to the store? For bananas?"

"Strawberries are fine," she says.

43. THE PARTY

LEWIS IS USED TO seeing strange cars in the driveway of the vacation rental next door, the closer of the two between his place and Gerry's. Every few days during spring and summer, a fresh SUV appears with kayaks strapped to the roof, or a Prius with a bike rack, or a minivan with four kids spilling out the automated sliding door. It's a small place, similar to the size of his: two bedrooms and one bath, with an extra pull-out futon in the living room. The listing allows up to six people to sleep there, but it's usually occupied by small families or couples. Especially couples. *The sex shack* is how he's come to think of it. There's a hot tub in the back, strings of lights around it, and a stone path down to a sandy beach on the river. It's just the kind of romantic place he imagined for himself and Veronica, and now he often hears a burst of laughter or playful squeals as a couple slip off their clothes and slide into hot bubbles. He's grateful the tub is far enough from his yard, with a high fence separating them, that he doesn't hear anything more.

This evening, though, when he and Sills return from a long hike—they went all the way up to the crest for the first time this summer, where a few patches of snow linger in shady spots, and mosquitoes swarmed them for four of nine miles—there's a huge camper van in the neighboring driveway, a dozen mountain bikes leaning against its side. And it sounds like more than a dozen voices coming from over the fence—laughing, shouting, hooting—along with loud music and pot smoke. He's not opposed to people having a good time, at least in theory, though tonight he's tired from the walk and the drive, and welts are already forming on his elbows and the backs of his knees despite the bug spray he'd slathered all over himself—first an organic one with citronella, and then the heavy-duty toxic DEET, neither of which warded off a single proboscis. Sills seemed unbothered by the insects and was generally awed on their walk. When they made it to a stunning meadow beneath Mount Washington where butterflies swooped over cat's ear and lupine, she sat on a stump staring at the scenery for twenty straight minutes without once telling him she was bored.

Now she's watching a movie she downloaded onto the iPad her mother bought her for her birthday, and she's equally unbothered by the noise from next door. Lewis wishes Gerry were here to tell the kids to shut up—maybe even to menace them with one of his many rifles—but he's away visiting one of his kids for most of the summer. In fact, he told Lewis he might not be coming back. As much as he loved being surrounded by timber and game, it was too lonely for him out here, and he was thinking about putting the place on the market in the fall. He asked for the name of Lewis's realtor. At the time, Lewis welcomed the news—no more leaf blowers and chainsaws—but he feels a slight pang now, imagining himself out here all winter by himself, the nearest real neighbor more than a mile downstream.

The temporary ones are growing louder, however, and when it's time for Sills to go to bed, he no longer hears voices because they've turned up their music to full volume. Not terrible music, at least—a dreamy sort of electronica, not too far afield from the droning rock he used to listen to in Portland clubs in his early twenties, swaying to a slow beat and staring at his shoes on a beer-sticky floor. But Sills yawns, says it was a great day, she hopes she'll dream about those butterflies, but how is she supposed to sleep with all that noise?

So he changes his sweaty shirt for a fresh one—long-sleeved, to keep him from scratching his elbows—and steps down the curve of gravel to the rental. He passes the camper and all the bikes—none of which are locked—and knocks on the front door. As he expects, there's no answer. Unlike his cabin, this one is a single-story simply built box with an aluminum roof. Purely functional, with concrete pavers not even meant to look natural, a plain cedar fence with a gate to the left of the attached garage. He knocks on this, too, but the music is so loud he'd have to hit it with a sledgehammer to have any hope of being heard. So, instead, he reaches over the fence, finds the latch, and eases the gate open.

Clouds of smoke mix with steam from the hot tub and drift over the string lights. He can't see anything beneath them yet, just tree trunks and ferns casting shadows at the edge of the yard. The smell is sweet, musky, and overpowering. He's already apologizing for intruding, though he doesn't yet know whom he's apologizing to. There are no voices, only music, and when he finally sees a face through the fog, its eyes are closed, hair hiding most of its face. And then others appear, similarly oblivious to his presence. The only sign that they are awake—or alive—is the slow bob of heads in rhythm with the pulsing beat.

He stands there for ten, fifteen seconds before one pair of eyes open, blink, and squint in his direction. He apologizes again, but a new drift of steam or smoke blocks the face before he can tell whether or not its owner hears him. Then others are coming alert, peering at him from lawn chairs and a picnic table, from inside the hot tub. And he calls louder, "Really sorry to bother you."

"Whoa," a voice says behind him, deep, slow, and stoned. "For a second I thought you were, like, a bear or something."

"Just the neighbor," he says. "Next door. My kid's trying to sleep."

"So sorry," says another voice, this one female and silky and closer than he expects. Closer, too, is the sound of the hot tub jets, just to his left. When he turns, he sees that the tub is full, six heads floating above churning water. One of them, with wet hair falling to shoulders and then disappearing beneath the surface, opens its mouth, and out comes the same silky voice. "I'll turn the music down."

Then the head rises, and where it was are suddenly a pair of small breasts, and then a wet triangle of dark hair. He turns away too late not to see what it partially hides, not to know he'll see it in his imagination for many days afterward. But what he realizes when he swivels, now that his eyes are adjusting to the dim light, is that the other faces staring at him through the swirling fog hover above more young bodies just as bare. Everywhere he looks are more breasts and buttocks and penises and swaths of hair he shouldn't see. So, instead, he gazes upward, at the serrated patch of sky between treetops, thousands of stars visible even though a sliver of moon has already risen above the horizon, a yellowish glow to the east. More than a year out here, and he is still awed each time he sees the sky clear of clouds and free of city lights. It's a week before the Perseid showers begin, and he's already seen two dozen meteors this summer. The sky is far more appealing, he tells himself, than all the lovely flesh that surrounds him.

"We're really sorry," the silky voice says again, louder than before. "We didn't mean to bother you."

Only now does he realize that the music has faded into the background, the beat no louder in his ears than his own pulse, which quickens when he sees the owner of the voice standing right in front of him. He focuses on her eyes, which are big and hazel, and the gap between her front teeth, behind which is a flash of tongue, rather than let himself glance any lower. But these things are no less alluring, no less likely to haunt his dreams.

"We had a long ride today. Just needed to unwind. It was thoughtless of us to imagine we're the only ones out here."

"I get it," he says. "I'm usually the only one out here. You can forget there's anyone around for miles."

"You live here full-time?" one of the naked boys asks, this one lounging in a hammock that rocks above a tall purple bong. "What a fucking dream."

"I'm all for people having a good time," Lewis says. "Glad you're enjoying our woods."

"I hope your kids can sleep now," says the girl with hazel eyes. "We'll keep it down the rest of the night."

"Just the one," Lewis says before he can stop himself. "My daughter. She stays out here with me on weekends."

"Tell her we're sorry."

"I'm sure she'll be out cold in a minute. We went on a long hike today. She was beat."

"Must be fucking silent out here during the week," says the boy in the hammock.

"Especially in the winter," Lewis says.

"I'd give my left nut," the boy says, "for a few days with nobody talking at me."

"Except not really silent," Lewis adds. "There's always the sound of the river. And you wouldn't believe how much wild-life shows up when no one's around. Owls hooting. Elk bugling in the hills."

"Sounds amazing," the girl says, but now her hazel eyes aren't in view. She's climbing back into the hot tub, and the seam of her ass briefly crosses his line of sight before lowering into the water. Steam swells around him. He thinks he might swoon. "You're welcome to hang out," she says. "There's beer inside. And, you know . . . if you partake."

"Help yourself," says the boy in the hammock, waving to the bong.

Lewis glances up again, hoping for what? To catch a meteor burning through the atmosphere? A sign for him to stay? A reminder that he'll never be twenty-four again, with a perfect, muscled body he never had the first time around?

"You all enjoy your evening."

He breathes in the smell once more—pot and chlorine and salty sweat—and heads for the gate.

44. BUBBLES

"JUST THOSE THREE ELEMENTS," her father says, floating on his back in the middle of the deep pool, only his face visible and the slight mound of his hairy belly.

"Whipped cream?" she asks as she swims to the big, flat rock, where she pulls herself up with difficulty, feet slipping once on the algae beneath the surface. She's scraped her knee here more than once and takes extra care climbing up now.

"Totally optional."

"Cherry?"

"Same."

"I don't believe it," she says, lying on her back, arms stretched above her head. Water drips from her sides, steams in the sun. She scans the sky for bald eagles—one passed overhead last week—but now it's just a perfectly empty strip of blue between the trees on either bank. Her legs are still chilled from the water, her fingers puckered and soft.

"That's what the article says."

"And who is this guy, the universal expert on all desserts?"

"Three elements: ice cream, sauce or syrup, and something crunchy."

"Doesn't even need to be nuts?"

There's moss under her head, a thick mat of it, as comfortable as any pillow. She remembered to put on sunscreen, a waterproof kind, so she doesn't have to worry about how long she stays out. She could stay here all day, all week, with the sound of the shallow rapids a hundred yards upstream, and birds, and her father's languid voice—easier today than usual, because he's not in any pain as he floats in the river, his back numbed by the cold water, buoyed by the gentle current.

"Pretzel pieces. They'll do the trick. Not the soft kind, of course. Rice Krispies. Crumbled Oreos."

"M&Ms?"

"Sure, I don't see why not. Crunchy enough. Especially when they're cold."

"What about, I don't know, croutons?"

"I suppose, if you want a disgusting one. Still a sundae."

"What about—"

"You want to know where they came from? Well, at least one theory?"

The backs of her eyelids are orange with sparkles of green. A drop of water hangs on one earlobe. She waits to see if it will dry up before it falls. She doesn't want to go back to town tomorrow. Her theater camp rehearsals ramp up this week, and she'll spend all her time memorizing lines and practicing her steps. She loves acting and dancing, but now she just wants to enjoy the release of summer, all demands evaporating from the skin of her shoulders and thighs where the bathing suit ends.

"Evolved from the ice-cream soda," he says. "The story goes that in some churchy bullshit town in the Midwest—"

"I hereby dedicate the town of Churchy Bullshit, Missouri."

"I think it was Illinois," he says. "But in any case, some churchy bullshit town council members, or maybe a mayor? They decided ice-cream sodas were too risqué for the Sabbath and banned anyone from selling them on Sunday."

"That is some churchy bullshit," she says, clamping down hard on the last syllable so it snaps between her teeth. One of the things she relishes most about being here is that she can swear as much as she wants without anyone telling her—as her mom always does—to make sure she curbs herself while she's at school. She knows how to curb herself plenty. What she wants is someone to encourage her to quit curbing so much, to say whatever the fuck she wants, which is what her father does when he's in the right mood, when he's not depressed or anxious or aching.

"So some clever soda fountain jerk—that's what they called themselves, soda jerks, because, I don't know, they jerked the lever on the fountain? He came up with an ice-cream soda without the soda."

"What the hell is an ice-cream soda anyway?"

"You never see them on the West Coast," he says. "I used to have them in New Jersey."

"That dump," she says.

"Your papa likes them."

"So they're super hip."

"Exactly."

"But what are they?"

"Like a root beer float. Except instead of root beer, it's got seltzer and chocolate syrup."

"No cherry?"

"So this guy decides to get around the churchy mayor's bullshit ban by making a new dessert. It's got ice cream, chocolate syrup, and to replace the bubbles in the soda, he adds something crunchy."

"Bubbles aren't crunchy."

"And because he serves it only on Sunday, he calls it a *Sunday*, only somewhere along the way it gets a creative misspelling and becomes a *sundae*, with an *e* at the end."

"Like Krispy Kreme."

"But all that might be an urban legend. Who knows."

"A churchy bullshit urban legend."

"Exactly."

He's pulled himself up beside her on the rock and sits, shivering, with his arms hugging his knees. Everything is too bright when she opens her eyes. The water eases past. "Do we have any ice cream?" she asks.

"A little, I think."

"Any chocolate syrup?"

"We can make some. Chocolate chips and milk. We've got those."

"Seltzer?"

"Doubt it."

"Ice-cream soda sounds refreshing. And we could stick it to all the churchy bullshitters."

"We've got peanuts. Almonds, too. All three elements for a sundae."

"Not the same as bubbles," she says and closes her eyes. He lies back beside her. No groan, only a little sigh. Water from his bathing suit rolls down a slant in the rock and cools the undersides of her knees. Neither of them moves for a long time.

45. REHEARSAL

SILLS HAS REHEARSALS ALL weekend, which means Lewis spends most of it driving back and forth into town. He picks up fast food for breakfast after dropping her off at the auditorium, where she'll run through her lines and dance steps twelve times on an empty stomach—because, she said, she was too nervous to eat. "You need sustenance," he said. "At least drink a lot of water. Supposed to hit a hundred today." He doesn't have enough time at the river to do much more than wade in and test out a few casts with a new fly before he has to get back in the car and wind his way down the canyon. On the way, he picks up more fast food for lunch—fries and a chicken sandwich he immediately regrets finishing—and to his surprise arrives before the kids have been let out. "They started late," another parent tells him. "Problems with the soundboard."

They're on the wide lawn in front of North Salem High School, standing in the shade of a huge sycamore maple which makes being outside bearable but doesn't keep him from sweating. He's spoken with this parent a number of times, the mother of one of the tech boys Sills complains about in a way that suggests they both annoy and intrigue her, with their big heads and feet and the beginning of fuzz on their upper lips, always joking and jostling and jockeying for attention. Their kids have been going to this theater camp together for the past three summers, and they've become familiar enough that they often drift toward each other during these interstitial moments. So much of parenting is standing around waiting, it seems, and he wonders how many hours he'll have spent this way by the time Sills goes away to college. The tech boy's mom knows his name, though he can't recall hers.

"I peeked for a second," she says. "Your girl was killing it."

Sills hasn't told him much about her part, only that it's a big one, though not exactly the lead—more like lead villain— and that she sucks at singing and wishes she could just dance. But he knows she's been working hard. The last two weekends she's done little other than practice while he's been fishing, taking breaks only to eat and cool off with dips in the river. As much as he hates musicals, he's enjoyed hearing her voice drifting to him on the water and feels a flush of pride as this mom—more attractive than he remembers, especially on a hundred-degree day, when she's in running shorts and a flimsy tank top—repeatedly praises her.

"She's been busting her tail," he says. "I've hardly gotten her to do anything else for the past month."

She smiles at him in a way that suggests admiration for his dedication as a father. He doesn't know her marital status, but he's never seen her with a husband, has never noticed her son—gangly and nearly as tall as Lewis, with auburn hair cut in a surfer's shag—picked up by a dad. Whether she's single or not, he finds the smile appealing, the narrow strip of teeth that appears between well-shaped lips, the way her eyes squint behind lavender-framed glasses. She chats about the ins and outs of the production, all the behind-the-scenes gossip. The director is stressed, she says; he depends on lots of ticket sales for funding, especially now that the school district requires him to match their contribution; one of his assistants is leaving after this year because she's pregnant; the parent volunteers have really stepped up this summer, and she thinks this performance will be their best ever. She's clearly more invested in the whole thing than her kid—who, according to Sills, plays video games on his phone during rehearsals and often misses his cues when all he's got to do is pull the curtain open and closed.

"It's been great, but I'll be glad when it's over," the tech boy's mom says. "We can finally enjoy some downtime. And get out of the heat. We're camping at Cape Lookout the day after the finale."

"Big family trip?" Lewis asks.

"Just the two of us," she says, and this time he thinks the smile is a little shy, or else perhaps a little embarrassed.

"We're doing the same," he says quickly, with a tone that's both proud and stoic, acknowledging the difficulties and pleasures of solo parenting. "Sills and I. Trying our first backpacking trip. Couple nights up in the Mount Jeff Wilderness."

"She's lucky."

"I just hope she can handle her pack. I don't know if my back can take carrying two."

She asks him where they'll hike, and he goes into too much detail about which trailhead they'll start from, which route they'll take to avoid the crowds at Marion Lake, where they'll set up camp. He's been looking at maps all summer, debating whether they should go for elevation or old growth, whether there will be too many mosquitoes still to risk sleeping near water. Even as he keeps talking, he worries about losing her attention—she clearly doesn't know the area he's talking about, the high plateau of lakes and buttes just to the west of the Cascade peaks—but after he finishes, she says, "I haven't spent enough time in the mountains. I'd like to do more." Beads of sweat hang on her eyebrows, and more are forming on her upper lip. He imagines the salty taste if he were to lick them off.

"Maybe next summer."

"This one's not over."

"That's true."

"And nothing beats the mountains in fall. Before the rain starts."

The doors to the auditorium pop open, and the first kids spill out. "You know," the mom says, and during a brief pause he imagines she's going to suggest they take their camping trip together—and already he's coming up with reasons not to, because of course as much as he might want to enjoy the company of this lovely mom in her tank top and shorts that show off muscled shoulders and thighs, he's been counting on this trip with Sills to solidify their bond in ways he can't yet imagine, giving them something they share with no one else. "If you didn't want to have to drive back and forth tomorrow," the mom continues. "I could pick up Skye on the way. We drive right past your place."

So maybe he has misunderstood the smiles after all. "Her mom's place," he says. "I'm way out in the country. You wouldn't want to have to carpool with me."

He expects this to put her off, but instead the smile returns, bolder now, more obvious. "Sorry," she says. "I had no idea. I've been divorced so long, I always think I'm the only one. So where do you live?"

He describes the cabin, the woods, the river, and the mom looks increasingly awed and eager.

"Wow," she says. "Sounds like a dream."

"Lot of driving," he says. "But Sills loves it out there. Keeps her off screens all weekend."

"God," she says. "That's exactly what we need."

"You'll have to come out and see it sometime," he says, and just then Sills is beside him, sweaty and pale and looking as if she might pass out.

"See what?" she asks.

"You haven't eaten anything, have you," he says. "Did you at least drink some water?"

"I'm tired," she says. "Can we go already?"

The tech boy's mom is waving to her son, who lopes down the path with head bent over his phone. Lewis calls goodbye to her, and he expects her to be too distracted to notice—if only he could remember her name—but to his surprise she turns to him and says, "I'd love to. Maybe after our camping trips." To Sills, she says, "Honey, you were on fire up there. You're gonna knock it out of the park next week."

Sills says nothing until they get into the car, which is so hot neither of them can sit. She fans herself with a hand while he runs the air-conditioning. "Why were you talking to Grant's mom?"

"Just being friendly," he says.

"You didn't invite them over, did you?"

"No, not really. Just telling her about our place."

"Not really?"

"It was just casual conversation. Told her about the cabin, and she said she'd like to see it."

"He's an idiot," she says and drops into the seat.

"Most boys are." He eases down beside her. The back of his shirt is soaked. The fabric of the seat sticks to his legs, and the steering wheel is still too hot to hold. "Before they turn twenty-three or so. Or maybe twenty-eight."

"No, I mean he's the dumbest kid on the whole crew."

"He can't be so bad."

"He always forgets his cues."

"His mom seems pretty smart. Even if she mixes metaphors."

"And he never knows where to set the props, even though the floor's marked."

"I mean, fire and baseball are both clichés. But at least stick with one."

"He walked into the girls' bathroom."

"Everyone makes mistakes."

"Like three times."

"Seriously? On purpose?"

"I don't know," she says.

"Did you tell the director?"

"Today he tripped and fell on Josie."

"On her?"

"His hands were on her boobs."

"Your mom hates that word."

"Breasts," she says.

"He's never coming to our place," he says, picturing, with a little pang, the mom's salty lips, the edge of her lace bra peeking out from her tank top when she lifted her arm to wave. "No chance. You don't have to worry about that."

46. SHARPAY

THE FINAL SHOW WENT as well as she could have hoped, and now she's exhausted. All she wants to do is go home, strip off her tights, and go to bed, but her parents have insisted on taking her out to celebrate. They're in an Italian place right next to the theater, and it's crammed with other kids from the production and their families. She's already said goodbye to many of them, given hugs—including two to Sebastian, who once again played the lead and got the longest and loudest applause—said she'll see them when school starts, or next summer for those who go to different schools, and now she has to smile at them again, and exchange further compliments, and let their mothers exclaim over how well her dance number went while they wait for a table to open. Her father actually remembered to make a reservation, which he has reminded them several times after the hostess told them it would be just a little longer. He grumbles about it now, shifting his weight from one foot to the other. "What's the point of a reservation if it doesn't actually reserve you anything?" he says.

"There's no rush," her mother says, without impatience. "I'm just glad we'll be able to toast you for all your hard work."

Her face hurts from smiling, and she can feel the stage makeup cracking on her cheeks. She's hungry, too, but the smell of garlic and grilled fish is too much for her right now, not without something to chew on. A waiter walks by with a basket of bread, and it takes all her restraint not to leap forward and grab a hunk. One of the younger kids from the theater camp spots her and shouts, "There's Sharpay! Look, it's Sharpay!"

Skye waves and wonders if she'll now always be known as the jealous, conniving character she played on stage—or if she could be that character for real, maybe, and constantly push to get whatever she wants. In the musical, of course, she ends up losing, but it doesn't work that way in actual life; if she were as assertive and manipulative as Sharpay, she'd have an easier time with most things. The key was not caring what other people thought of you.

But the only people she knows who don't care what others think are boys like Grant Skelding, who comes into the restaurant with his mom and stands right next to her in the waiting area without even acknowledging her. They've worked on this show together all summer, and he hasn't said a word about her performance, not once, and she hates that she wants him to look up and say *nice job* or something equally meaningless. Anything would be better than his complete indifference. His mother coos over her, tells her parents how wonderful she was, how proud they must be, but she has a weird, stunned look as she speaks, and Skye wonders if she's as stupid as her son. It troubles her to think that people who otherwise look put together, even elegant, can be straight-up morons.

She's lucky, at least, that the hostess has Grant's table ready, and they don't have to share the same space for more than a minute. He shuffles past her, and she hates it just as much that she finds something captivating about his shambling stride, the ruffle of his shaggy bangs. His mother says, "Bye, honey, great job. Bye, Lewis," and Skye catches her father making an odd, closed-lip smile that looks sort of like a sneer, and her mother's eyes dart to the side for just a second. She pretends not to have noticed either. Then her father's grumbling again about their table not being ready, about other people walking right in and sitting down, and her mother, less patient now, says, "Two-tops are always easier to find."

"You're right, I should have worn a tube top," her father says, and for a second she isn't sure if he really heard wrong. But of course he's joking, trying to ease the tension by hamming it up, sticking out his hip and saying, "What, don't you think I'd look good in a tube top? I could be Sharpay next year," which is enough to make her mother smile, if not laugh, and then finally the hostess leads them to their table.

This is the first time Skye has been together with both parents for more than a few minutes since the split, and they are both working hard to show how normal it is, how they can still be a family in this new configuration. Neither wants to step on the other's toes by sitting next to her, so they sit next to each other across the table from her, which seems anything but normal, their shoulders just a few inches apart, their postures stiff and formal, their smiles strained. She just wants to get it over with as quickly as possible, so she picks up the menu right away, scans through for something familiar—lasagna, green salad— and asks if she can get some bread. Her father tries to flag down a waiter, but she flies past without noticing. Her mother gushes some more about the show, says she must be ready for a break, asks if she's excited about having a whole week at the cabin.

"What do you two have planned?" she asks, in a voice that's attempting to be cheerfully neutral, as if she hasn't already asked Skye for all the details, as if it's all the same to her what they do.

Her father in turn talks about the backpacking trip he's been cooking up for a month to some lake she's never heard of beneath Mount Jefferson, where they can hike up to a butte with a view over the whole Cascade Range, from Rainier to Shasta—all of which sounded exciting to Skye when she first heard about it, though now, after hearing about it for the twentieth time, just sounds tedious and taxing. Like sitting in this stupid restaurant, waiting for someone to bring her one stupid piece of bread.

"Sounds wonderful," her mother says with that same false cheer, though maybe it's more false now, easier to see through—hear through—especially during the long pause before she asks, "You've mapped out your route?"

"It's pretty straightforward," her father says. "Up past Red Lake, and onto the PCT."

"I mean, I wouldn't want you getting lost out there."

"Just two trails," he says. "Pretty hard to get lost."

"It's the wilderness," she says and then gives a little laugh that's more genuine than anything she's said so far. "And it's you."

"We'll stay on the trails," he says and picks up his menu. Her mother still hasn't looked at hers, though she's always the one who needs the most time to decide what she wants. "That only happened once," he adds.

"Once is plenty."

"And we found our way back in a few hours."

"Not a big deal if we had any food. Or water."

"We survived."

"You have a filter this time?"

"Of course I do."

"And bug spray? Mosquitos could still be brutal this time of year."

"I've got it," he says.

"And you checked the fire map? No closures in that part?"

"Ronnie," he says.

"I know there's something near the Metolius."

"It's nowhere near where we'll be," he says, and Skye feels herself growing dizzy with hunger now, the noise of people talking and dishes clattering in the open kitchen too loud in her ears, silverware catching the light of candles and flashing in her periphery. The waiter appears, and she orders quickly, forgetting to ask for her salad dressing on the side, but it doesn't matter, as long as they bring her some bread soon. Her father asks for the hanger steak rare, which she knows will cause him to hunch over the toilet in the middle of the night and, in the morning, pretend he slept just fine despite blood-shot eyes. Only then does her mother pick up her menu, and she asks question after question about dishes Skye knows she won't order—whether she could get the salmon without the creamed corn, whether the duck breast is on the dry side— before settling on the chicken cacciatore, which is what Skye knew she'd get all along. And then, before the waiter walks away, she says, "Wait. Honey, don't you want your dressing on the side?"

And before she can stop herself, Skye says, "I just want some fucking bread. Can I get some fucking bread before I fall over, please?"

Her parents stare at her. So does the waiter. She smiles. Her cheeks ache.

"That was Sharpay," she says. "I'm still in character."

Her father claps, too loudly. The waiter hurries off.

Her mother blinks away tears. "I'm just going to miss you, that's all. You know that, right?"

47. SOUR

THEY'VE FORAGED ALL SPRING and summer: for thimbleberries, black caps, fiddlehead ferns, the tiny wild strawberries that grow along the sides of trails, nettles they harvest with gloves on before blanching to make a pesto. Nothing excites Sills more than improvising a meal out of what they've found in the forest, and though these meals leave Lewis famished, he encourages her because she's more likely to eat a full plate if it's something she's prepared. She's always been a picky eater, ever since she was an infant and nearly choked on a cracker in the shape of a rabbit on the run. After that, he and Veronica were overly careful with what they fed her, and she started turning her nose up at anything unfamiliar. "Everyone fucks up their first kid," Veronica said at the time, before they decided one was all they'd have. Now Sills won't eat a pizza if it's got too much sauce or a potato if someone has cracked a peppercorn over it. He sometimes worries she won't survive on her own when the time comes, so it's a comfort to see her devour the mashed tuber of a camas lily after learning that's what indigenous people in the region ate for thousands of years. He found the tuber tasteless and chalky, even with extra butter and salt, and not filling enough, and after she went to bed, he snuck to the refrigerator for some leftover chili.

Today all they manage to gather are oxalis leaves and red huckleberries. Unlike the blue variety, the latter are tiny and tart, and most people leave them to wither on the plant. But Sills says they're her favorite, spends an hour picking to fill a single plastic container the size of her fist. The oxalis is plentiful at this elevation, and he always enjoys the first release of its juice between his molars, though after a leaf or two, he's satisfied. But Sills stuffs a gallon-sized freezer bag full of them, and when they get home, she sets to work making a salad. Lewis already knows he's going to be hungry for the rest of the evening, but he calls enthusiastically from the front room, "Almost ready? I can't wait to eat it."

"Just finishing the dressing," she says. "Don't we have any lemons?"

"You used them all. There's a bottle of concentrate in the pantry."

He smells fish cooking, which is a good sign—maybe he won't end up ravenous after all. Still, he'll likely need a late-night snack, especially since hunger exacerbates his sleeplessness, guarantees he'll stare up at the ceiling for hours.

"You found the trout? I bought it from an old geezer up in Gates." When she doesn't answer, he says, "Fresh caught on Thursday. Doesn't need much for flavor. A quick pan grilling, and it'll be perfect."

"Who's cooking here?"

"He sells them right out of his backyard. Always has a dozen or so in a cooler. Says they're fly-caught, but I don't believe him. Pretty sure he's got an illegal net upriver."

"Blackened black market fish," she says.

"Good thing ethics don't spoil taste."

Everything looks beautiful when she sets it on the table. She's seared the fish with the huckleberries, which have popped and given it a pinkish glaze. There are more berries in the salad, which is otherwise mostly made up of oxalis leaves, along with a few slices of carrot and a chopped tomato. He takes a bite, and his mouth instantly puckers.

"Lemon juice in the dressing," he says.

"And a little white vinegar."

"You know, oxalis is also called sour grass," he says.

"I'm the one who told you that."

"It's terrific," he says and takes a bite of trout, which is even more sour. "Lemon in here, too," he says.

"Yup," she answers. She sticks a big forkful of salad in her mouth, chews slowly, and does her best not to make a face. She says nothing more, just stares at him in defiance. He responds with an equally big mouthful of fish, forces his eyes to stay open, though everything in him is trying to close down to bear it. He swigs some wine, but it tastes bitter. He switches to water, and that, too, tastes wrong, as if he forgot to rinse the soap out of the glass last time he washed it.

Sills is still glaring at him when he sets it down. He takes another bite, and so does she. Neither of them is going to bend. It has become an unspoken challenge, no longer a meal but a duel. They trade bite for bite, and Lewis doesn't let up even when he can feel the inside of his mouth going raw from all the acid. He'll have canker sores by tomorrow, but he's not going to show her he can't take it, and of course neither will she. They finish what's on their plates. They take seconds. He's actually getting full, but he doesn't stop until he spears the last huckleberry from the salad bowl and splits it with his front teeth. Sills looks pale but satisfied. She takes a gulp of water and cringes.

"Maybe we need some lemonade," he says.

"Good idea." She goes to the kitchen, comes back with two glasses. He knows before he takes a sip that she's given him iced lemon water with no sugar added. He guzzles it down.

"Hungry for dessert?" he asks.

"Wish we could make lemon bars," she says. "But we don't have any cream."

"We can drive to the store."

"And maybe some Sour Patch Kids." She gives him that look of provocation again, daring him to say enough's enough.

"I'll grab the keys," he says. "Find your shoes."

48. JEANS

WHEN SHE WAS A little kid, maybe four or five years old, she asked her father why she had brown eyes like his when her mother's were blue. The answer she heard was, "You've got some of my jeans, some of hers. We stitched them together to make you." And what she pictured was each of her parents tearing off a leg from their jeans and sewing them together—her mother's leg shorter and slimmer and fresher than her father's, who wore his jeans loose and faded and sometimes torn—so they wouldn't fit anyone. What did a ghastly, unusable pair of pants have to do with her eyes?

Now, even though she understands the basic principle of genetics well enough, has learned what happens between sperm and egg, she still pictures that ugly pair of jeans whenever she thinks about what she's inherited from each of her parents. From her father, for example, the tendency to assume everything will turn out well even when evidence suggests otherwise. And from her mother, a desire to anticipate the future, plan for contingencies, and worry when those plans aren't in place.

"It's getting thicker," she calls to her father, who's twenty feet downstream. He's standing close to the middle of the river, where the current is strongest, but even there the water reaches only to just above the knees of his waders. She's never seen it so low and can't reconcile the sight of it with her memories from the past winter and spring, when it nearly topped the bank, which is over her head. Everything is impossibly dry now, the yard covered in chalky gravel dust from the road, the air full of smoke from the fires near the crest. They postponed their backpacking trip the week before last because fire crews closed the road to the trailhead to use as a staging area; her father assured her it would reopen this weekend, but instead, more lightning strikes hit nearby, closing much of the wilderness area, and now they plan to camp in the yard instead. But so much smoke has drifted down the canyon, she isn't sure they'll be able to stay out all night. They won't be able to see any stars either way, which was supposed to be the highlight of the trip—a new moon and the Perseid meteor shower at its peak. "Do you think we should head out?"

"The wind'll turn," he insists, though how he knows this he doesn't say. He swings his rod, and the yellow line makes its graceful snake shapes in the air over his head before sailing forward and landing in an eddy near the far bank. In a year and a half, she has yet to see him catch a fish, though he claims he's landed a few during the week, when he fishes in the evening after work, all too small to keep. She knows the point is simply to be out here, to be waving his arms and feeling the water pushing against his legs. That's all she wants, too: right now, she's perfectly content beneath a section of bank that overhangs the beach, with roots poking through dirt overhead, where she whittles sticks into spears. Or she would be, if it weren't for the damn smoke that turns everything hazy and strange and makes her nose and throat itch. "It'll clear by tonight," her father says, even though she can hardly see him now. His voice, too, seems to come from farther away, muffled by the sound of water.

"Are you sure the fire won't come here?" she asks. "Don't you think we should load up the car just in case?"

"The closest hot spot is twenty-five miles away," he says. "If it came this direction, we'd have plenty of warning."

His reassurances are full of certainty, which only troubles her more. Floating in the air in front of her are little bits of white ash, all that's left of trees high up in the mountains. They move like snowflakes, and she expects them to feel cool when she reaches out and grabs them. But they're no colder or hotter than the hot air around them, and they smear with her sweat into a grayish grime on her palm. She goes back to whittling her stick with the knife her father had in his tackle box, so dull it wouldn't have sliced a strawberry before she sharpened it.

"I'm just saying, it might be worth getting ready. In case we need to move in a hurry," she calls.

"We're in the wettest part of the range," he says. His voice is closer now, but she can't see him at all. The point of her stick is angled gently on three sides, but the fourth she can't get quite right and keeps blunting the tip. "No fires have burned these woods for a thousand years."

Even at the river's edge, it doesn't seem like a wet place. On the exposed rocks are tufts of dried algae, stiff and brittle for weeks. When she takes a big breath, her throat burns, and she has to work hard not to cough.

By evening, the smoke hasn't cleared, and there's no chance

of seeing the Perseids, so they stay inside, running a pair of box fans pointing out the windows to keep the cabin clear, but all they do is bring more smoke in through the vents in the roof.

"Maybe we should seal it up instead?" she asks.

"It's just because of an inversion," he says. "The hot air gets trapped on the ground. Usually doesn't last more than a few days."

"It's been almost a week."

"We just got unlucky. We'll camp next weekend. Plenty of summer left. Fall's great for being out, too."

"It's hurting my eyes," she says.

"Do you want me to take you back to your mom's?" His voice has that brittle, wounded quality she knows should make her feel pity but always enrages her instead. "I'm sure she'd understand."

"I just want you to close the damn windows."

"It'll pass soon," he says, pulling a fan away and shutting a sash. Then he hurries across to the opposite window. He's wearing shorts, but she pictures those loose jeans he wears all winter, the ones whose legs swish against each other when he walks. They're worn and soft and look as comfortable as sweatpants, and sometimes she wishes she wore a pair like them instead of the tight ones that hug her hips and thighs and match her mother's and her friends'.

"I know it will," she says and wants to believe it herself. But the itch in her nose is too intense, and before she can stop it, a sneeze rocks her forward and fills her hands with gritty, ash-colored snot.

49. THE ROCK

THE WORST PART IS the sound. He can close his eyes and block the view, but even with his hands over his ears, he can't shut out the roar that rattles his head, like being stuck inside a jet engine at thirty thousand feet. It covers the rippling water and the gusting east wind and his pounding pulse. It would cover his daughter's screams, too, if she weren't silent beside him in the water, watching the flaming trees on the bank. They're hanging on to the wide, flat rock in the middle of the river, and the only thing keeping them, too, from going up in smoke is the deep pool around them, three yards on either side. When the heat gets too intense, they take turns dunking heads, hanging on to each other's hand to make sure they don't slip into the current and drift away. When they come up, steam instantly rises from their hair.

An hour ago he woke to the sound of crackling. The smell of smoke was strong in his nose, but he'd gotten used to that over the past two weeks, an inversion keeping the stagnant air stuck in the canyon, waiting for the wind to shift direction. But instead it only picked up speed, whipped harder from the east, over the mountains from the high desert, not a drop of moisture in it. During the night it streaked the spot fires quickly down the ridges and along the canyon floor, and now it surrounds them on all sides.

Sills hasn't said a word since he roused her and told her they needed to leave. By the time they stepped outside, the road was hardly visible. Burning logs crossed it in both directions, and the brush on the other side was a solid blanket of fire. They ran to the river instead, skirting smoking ferns and scrambling down the bank. Both of them were barefoot, wearing nothing but what they'd worn to bed—Lewis, boxers and a T-shirt; Sills, underwear and a pajama top. Only when his feet hit the water did he realize their bottoms had burned, and the pain made him cry out. He guessed Sills must have felt the same pain, but no sound emerged from her as they ran over stones until they reached the pool and swam to the rock, not a groan or a sigh or a whimper.

So, instead, he fills the void with words that sound meaningless to him even as they spill out of his mouth, though they are better than the thunderous clamor of a burning world: "We can stay here all night. We can stay as long as we need to. This rock isn't going anywhere. It was here before any of the houses, any of the trees. It'll be here after we're all gone. As long as we hang on to it, we're okay. The water will keep us cool. If we get too cold, all we need to do is pull ourselves out for a minute. Nothing can get us here."

He wants some response from her, something other than her blank stare in the direction of the cabin, which isn't discernible through the orange wall and screen of smoke. He worries her eyes will suffer damage from looking straight at the fire, as if she's gazing right into the sun. It must be two in the morning, but it's as bright as midday. Upstream fifty yards, where a flaming thicket of salmonberry canes leans over the bank, water near the edge bubbles. But here it's still cool. This water traveled from underground springs and glacier-melt and no amount of sunshine or fire can take the chill out of it. He feels himself shivering even as the heat sears his neck.

"Time for another dunk," he says. "And then we'll get out and warm up for a minute."

Sills's fingers are white and pruned against the black rock. His own are cramping. He digs them harder into a crease. The only thing he needs to do is not let go. It's his only job, his only purpose in life. He keeps his grip with his right hand and takes Sills's wrist with his left. She draws a breath and goes under. This pure water, so clear he can see the top of her head as it bobs well beneath the surface. He won't let it out of his sight, won't let go of her wrist no matter how hard the current pulls. She comes up coughing—the first sound she's made in, what, an hour since they ran out of the house? Two?—though he can't really hear it over the incessant snarl of the flames, only feels the vibration in his hand and sees the way it bucks her body forward.

He puts an arm around her waist and lifts her onto the rock, where she drips and steams into the pocks made by bubbles of hot gas so many million years ago when the lava it came from cooled. His eyelids sting, his cheeks, the inside of his nostrils. He lowers himself into the water, a sheath of ice over his skin, and he lets himself stay there because he knows it's the only thing that fire can't touch. It can take everything from him, the car, the cabin, the forest, but it can't take the river, and because he needs something to hold on to so badly, he'll have to hold on to that.

Except now he's forgotten to hold on to the rock, and when he pushes up, he's drifted away from it. Not more than a few feet, but Sills is kneeling at its edge, shouting, the first words she's said all night. He can't hear them, the sound swallowed by the fire, consumed like the fuel on the ground and the oxygen in the air, torn apart and reconfigured as carbon dioxide and ash, but as he swims back to her, he can see the shape her mouth makes, lips pulling back, teeth opening wide, and when he reaches the rock and touches his hands back to the surface smoothed by millions of gallons of water rushing over it for millions of years—so smooth it's hard to find a place to grab, but he finally does, locking his fingers into a notch just below her—he knows she's shouting the only word he needs to hear: "Dad! Dad! Dad!"

50. JUST US

THE DOCTORS TREAT HER like an infant and won't tell her
anything, but her mother, as usual, has explained in more detail
than she needs: the injuries are a combination of thermal and
chemical, and the toxins have gotten into her bloodstream.
That's why it's still hard for her to breathe and why she still has
an IV hooked up to her arm. But the damage to her lungs is less
extensive than they first feared, and though she may always
have reduced capacity, before too long she'll start to feel almost
normal, and she can resume regular activities. "Exercise will be
good for it, to build your strength back," her mother says. "So
you don't have to worry about not being able to dance when
you're ready."

"When can I go home?" she asks, her voice raspy and thin
but more audible than it's been for days.

She's been in the hospital a week already, and every time
she asks how much longer, her mother says, "As soon as I know,
I'll tell you. I promise."

The only thing about which her mother has been less

forthcoming is how her father is doing. Whenever Skye asks, her mother's face goes rigid with anger and frustration before she forces it into a neutral expression. Skye knows she blames him for having her there when the fire swept through, for not listening to the news reports that warned of the east winds and the danger they might bring, and knows she's also frustrated because she can't really blame him or anyone else, understands that no one could have predicted how fast the fire was going to spread, how hot it would burn. The subsequent news reports she's watched on her hospital room's TV and read on her phone have all called it unprecedented, another example of how unprepared everyone is for climate change, how even the experts didn't see this coming, though perhaps the authorities should have known to evacuate people ahead of time, and certainly the power company should have turned off electricity to lines that blew down and sparked new blazes. She's seen the maps that show how much area the fire covered and its intensity, and all of them suggest that the canyon got the worst of it.

She knows the cabin is likely gone, and all the trees she has loved so deeply, and if she thinks about it too much she'll start crying again, which only makes her chest ache more. Outside the air has finally cleared of the smoke that filled the whole valley for days. A layer of ash dusts the windowsill beside her bed. Everyone keeps telling her how lucky she is, how wise she and her father were to take refuge in the river. If they'd tried to drive out, they would have died for sure. Some of their neighbors did.

"How's Dad today?" she asks now, and her mother gets that exasperated look once more—a look, at least, that tells Sills he's alive and out of real danger. "Is he able to get up yet?"

"He can hardly talk, but he keeps trying to make jokes about his sexy voice. And sing Tom Waits songs."

Skye laughs, but it hurts her throat and makes her cough. By the time they finally left the river, she was delirious, and she remembers only her father muttering incomprehensibly as he draped her over his shoulder and carried her up the bank and across a blackened landscape, a few trees still on fire but most only smoldering, and then down the road to the highway, where someone—an ambulance? Just a passing car? She can't remember—picked them up and drove them to the emergency room. This much she's managed to pry out of her mother: her father had third-degree burns on the bottoms of both feet, and he shredded one of them to pulp on river rocks and gravel; the nerves were so damaged he didn't even notice while he was walking, but now he's had skin grafts and hasn't yet been able to get out of bed. It'll be at least another week before he can walk at all. It's hard for Skye to imagine the possibility that he won't go hiking again, won't be able to trudge over boulders or stand in a river fishing. She can't imagine doing these things without him, but then the places where they did them, too, are no longer what they were and never will be again.

"What is it, sweetie?" her mom asks, which is how she knows she's crying. But it's too painful, like opening little cuts in her throat and lungs, so she closes her eyes, and soon she's asleep. When she wakes, her father's in the room with her, in a wheelchair, his legs propped up on some kind of stirrups, bandaged to the shins. His face is deep red, as if from a sunburn, and his hair is newly shorn, with a bald patch on the right side that makes him look either deranged or comical. He otherwise appears bright-eyed, a little manic, even, and she thinks she understands why: he can't believe they're still here. It's absurd that so much could get reduced to cinders, and this nondescript gray-haired man and his skinny daughter could come out with nothing but charred feet and scorched lungs that nevertheless keep air moving in and out.

"Next, let's try a tornado," he says, and his voice sounds even worse than she expected, like he's gargling glass splinters.

"How about a tsunami?"

"Hurricane would be too easy. Unless maybe it's a category five."

"Earthquake would be good. There's supposed to be a big one in the next, I don't know, fifty to a hundred years?"

"I'm not sure I can wait that long."

"Volcano," she says. "Next time we know one's gonna blow, we'll climb to the top and race the lava down."

"Perfect," he says.

The smile makes her face sting, so she forces it down, and it must be the lowering of her lips that makes her ask, "Did you see it on the way out?"

"I couldn't really tell where we were. I think we came onto the road near Gerry's."

"Was his place okay?"

"If okay means completely obliterated."

"He wasn't there, was he?"

"No. In Boise with his kids."

"Do you think any of it's left?"

"I doubt it, kiddo. Just us."

"What now?" Her voice is reaching its limit. She knows she doesn't have many words left before she'll need to go quiet again. "Where?"

"Now? I'm going to take advantage of this institution's wonderful hospitality. And high-quality liquid diet. And maybe I'll get to walk out of here with you soon. That would be enough, don't you think?"

She agrees but can't say it, so she only nods.

"I can't believe what I got you into," he says, quieter now, his voice a growl. "I wish I could say I'll never let anything bad happen to you again. But shit. Last person who can claim that."

"Shut up," she says, though it pains her, and she isn't sure he can hear.

Then he starts singing a song, something about being east of East Saint Louis, and about wind and rain, in a tune she almost recognizes, though she can't place it now. Then his voice, too, fades out, and they just watch each other without speaking. She listens to his shuddering breath until she can't tell it apart from her own.

51. RUINS

HE ISN'T SUPPOSED TO drive yet, nor walk more than a few steps at a time, but the doctors have sent him away with boot-like soft casts that make it easy to press the gas and brake and to hobble around with the help of a cane. The nerves haven't grown back yet, either—if they ever will—so he doesn't feel any pain in his soles, only where the burns stopped, halfway up his feet and on the tops of his toes. He's borrowed a car from his coworker, and he and Sills drive the familiar route out of town. He told her she wouldn't want to see the place in its current state, that she should probably stay home, and as expected, she said, without the slightest hesitation, "I'm coming." Her mother, too, tried to object, but only half-heartedly. They both knew there was no chance Sills would do anything but what she wanted.

It's strange how untouched it all looks for the first twenty miles, how everyone goes about their days as if nothing has happened. People pick peaches in the orchard just past the prison, horses graze in a yellow field, white oaks look parched but still hold their gnarled branches and glorious crowns to the unrelenting sun. Only when they reach the wide mouth of the canyon and the highway begins to climb do they start to see signs that their world has really changed, that they didn't dream it all. The first sooty trunks and blackened undergrowth, and then higher, full stands of burned trees, a charred pickup abandoned on the side of the road. The diner is gone, as if a bomb took it down to its foundation, and so is the ranger station at the crossroads where they turn off to follow the river.

A mile in, they come to a roadblock: a pair of sheriffs' cars with lights twirling. Lewis has to show an old electrical bill to get past, one he left at Veronica's house back when they owned the cabin jointly; only residents are being let through, escorted by a Forest Service truck so someone can keep an eye out for hazard trees. "Just an hour," one of the deputies tells him. "Load up anything you can save. But don't go walking near any stumps or snags. Roots can still be burning down there. Upward of three thousand degrees. Enough to melt you right into glass."

He keeps looking over to see how Sills is taking it all in, expects her to gasp when she recognizes a missing house or a meadow turned to coals, but she just stares out the window, taking big breaths as her doctors have encouraged to regain her lung capacity. They pass the golf course he never paid attention to except as a marker that he was only ten minutes from home. The greens are still green, flags waving above holes, sand traps inviting as a sunny beach. Only the clubhouse is gone, a row of burned-out carts in the parking lot beside its remains. And from there the sights only get worse: almost no green in the canopy, none in the underbrush, an unending stretch of black and brown until they turn onto gravel. Here, fallen trees have been shoved aside just enough to make a path through the middle of the road, one lane only, and where once their view of the river was blocked, they can see straight down to the water, where it drops over a shallow ledge and foams. He expects it, too, to have blackened, but it remains clear, blue-tinted, as fresh as always, though it carries more debris than usual, bringing rich nutrients to the unburned fields of the valley below.

Or so at least he consoles himself when they turn the corner and see the open space where Gerry's house once stood, only the stone fireplace still rising above the scorched earth like the keep of an ancient castle, besieged but never breached. The first vacation rental between them is now just a set of concrete steps leading to nothing. He pumps the brakes, lets them slow just shy of a full stop, asks, "Are you sure you want to see it?"

"I didn't get to say goodbye," Sills says.

He eases his foot off the pedal and rolls them up the hill another fifty yards. And there it is, the emptiness he expected, though so much worse than he could have imagined, because he remembers exactly where the huckleberry bushes he transplanted should have been, even though now there's not a trace of them; exactly where the wooden rake, now decimated, hung in the garden shed now reduced to a few chrome brackets and hooks and a buckled aluminum roof. And his car, a shell of steel, twisted in spots as if it writhed in pain as the flames overtook it, the windshield shriveled on one side but intact, a sticky patch of goo where one of the tires had been.

And the house itself? It's hard to believe how little evidence remains of the nearly two years he spent here, the weekends with Sills, the lonely weeknights on his own, which now fill him only with nostalgia rather than anguish. Here is the line of the foundation, and in its center, the stout black woodstove, unscathed. He wishes he'd thought to store valuables in it, like a safe, though what would have been valuable enough to bother with? His wallet and cell phone? His fishing rod? The wedding ring he couldn't bring himself to give away? What did any of those things matter?

Sills picks her way through rubble, turning over what must have been the door of the dryer. She bends down, grabs something, holds it up. It's white, but from far away he can't tell what it is. She waves it around, and it looks like a surrender flag, only skinnier, with straps at each end. Definitely fabric. "Got what I needed," she calls. "Now I can get on with my life."

Only when he gets closer does he see: a bra. "Any of my boxers in there?" he asks. "If I wear this pair another day, they'll fuse to my butt."

From the road, the Forest Service employee calls out the window of his truck, "Another ten minutes, and we've got to head out."

Sills finds a few treasures to stuff into her backpack. Her collection of geodes, a pocketknife, a mysterious hunk of metal they decide to identify later. Lewis doesn't know if he should bother salvaging anything. There are forks and spoons, broken plates, the old Remington typewriter he bought at a junk store a decade ago and never used. His records melted together, no music left in their grooves. Eventually he'll have to clean it all up so his detritus doesn't blight the landscape more than necessary, but there's no time now. They'll come back in the spring, search for morels in the scorched yard, clear away all the traces they left. Sills hasn't asked yet if they'll rebuild, but if she does, he's been ready to tell her he doesn't know. It could be years before they'd be allowed to return, but he's already decided to let it go, give this space back to whatever might regrow here, back to the river to pass through as it has for so long. He won't sell the land, won't let anyone else build on it, will only consider the time he spent on it borrowed, now returned.

"Look," Sills says and gestures toward a corner of the yard. "That tree made it."

It isn't the big Doug fir with the split trunk but a younger one, maybe thirty, maybe fifty years old, more than a foot in diameter, singed at the base but untouched above, still green at the crown.

"The new queen," Sills says. "May she long rule over the land. Or long may she rule. Whatever. You get the idea."

"Do you want to go down?" Lewis says. "Say a proper goodbye?"

"Can you make it on those?" she asks, glancing at his casts, the rubber end of his cane, all now covered in soot.

"I'll manage. Just stay clear of any trunks. Remember what he said about burning roots."

"Time to go!" the Forest Service employee calls.

They ignore him, make their way down the unfinished flagstone path dusted with ash, ease over the bank and onto the rocky beach. A big black log bobs in the deep pool beside the rock where they spent the night.

"We should camp there again," Sills says.

"Maybe some night when it's not so hot."

She kicks off her shoes and steps into the shallows. "Feels good," she says.

"Wish I could join you."

She crouches down, cups water in both hands. For a moment he thinks she's going to take a sip and is ready to warn her as he did when they first came to the river: not safe to drink, risk of parasites, always have to filter or boil it first. But then she jumps up and flings her arms in his direction. Above them, a flash of devious smile. The water splashes across his chin and neck and chest, drips down to his belly and under the waistband of his jeans, a shock of cold that makes him gasp air into his tattered lungs.

52. THE SLAB

HER MOTHER HAS CHANGED clothes in the last hour. Not as formal as what she wears to work, not revealing too much, but not what Skye is used to seeing her wear at home. Fresh jeans that hug her hips, a crisp black shirt with cap sleeves and a V-neck that stops just short of cleavage. A little makeup too. Subtle eye shadow, lipstick. Earrings. A silver necklace with a small pendant, a blue-green gem at her throat.

"It's none of your business," she says when Skye asks where she's going, with whom. "It isn't anyone's business."

"Didn't Dad give you that necklace?"

"He also gave me you."

"But you don't wear me out on dates."

"You two have fun. Or whatever," her mother says. "It's the weekend. I'm not here. You're not here. You're in the woods."

When she leaves, Skye passes through the pantry into the garage, which she and her father have been calling *the town cabin*, or sometimes *home on the slab*. He's been living in it for two weeks, and though he's said he'll move into an apartment nearby once he gets the first insurance check to pay the deposit, it's hard for Skye to imagine how he'll live on his own any- time soon. Now that his casts are off, he has trouble walking farther than from the love seat they bought at Goodwill to the camp bed set up beside the water heater. It'll be another month before he can drive. Her mother drops him off at work in the mornings while Skye walks to the bus stop and rides to school. He eats dinner with them in the evening before retreating to the garage, which is still warm enough now even at night, though by the start of October he won't be able to sit out here without a space heater.

By then he'll be gone, he says whenever she brings it up, so she doesn't have to worry about him freezing. The truth is she doesn't want him to go. She's gotten attached to this new arrangement and hopes to prolong it, for at least a few more weeks or maybe a few more months—or, really, until she goes away to college, if she had her choice. "Your family's even more fucked up than mine," June said when she finally healed enough to go back to school and told her friends how they were managing now. For the first few days, Skye clung to the delu- sion that her parents might get back together now that they saw each other every day, but it didn't take long to see her mistake. Her mother no longer looks at her dad with anything close to romantic feelings. Tolerance, yes, even affection. She laughs at some of his jokes, shakes her head at most. And her dad, too, finally seems to need nothing from her other than their brief banter and gentle taunts. They're just old friends now, and Skye has decided that's far preferable to being a married couple who share a bed and expectations they—or at least one of them—can never meet.

She drops into the love seat beside him. They've made the space as cozy as possible for a concrete pad surrounded by unpainted drywall, one side lined with metal shelving crammed with old paint cans, coiled garden hoses, plastic sleds they hardly ever used. Along with the love seat are a side table and kitchen chair, a pair of rugs—one from Skye's room, one from her mother's office—a wooden chest to hold the few outfits he's bought to replace all those that burned. On one of the rugs Skye has made her own bed for weekends, with a blow-up mattress, a pillow and sleeping bag, a stuffed monkey she hasn't wanted to sleep without since the fire. She squeezes it whenever she wakes up from terrible dreams, bites down on its floppy arm, throttles its stupid smiling face.

"Feel like playing poker?" she asks. "Or starting a new puzzle?"

"We could just go inside and watch a movie."

"I like it out here," she says.

"If only an inferno hadn't destroyed your tablet. Do you happen to know the passcode on your mom's?"

"Screen's too small," she says. "The TV comes off the wall pretty easy. Just hooked onto the mount."

"I guess that makes it mobile. There's an open outlet behind the tool bench."

"Will the cable reach out here?"

"Oh yeah. No problem."

They carry the TV together, her dad shuffling carefully over the tiles, occasionally wincing. Despite his pain, she can't help cackling as they leave the living room and squeeze sideways through the narrow pantry. "Mom's going to be so pissed," she says.

"We're just borrowing it," her father says.

"She'll be furious."

"I know."

She thinks of other things they could borrow: the living room armchair, the kitchen table, the microwave. Her mother's bed too. They could move the whole house out here, and all three of them could live on the slab. Or all four: Verlaine has already taken to the idea, slipping in ahead of them and sprawling across the middle of the love seat.

"Who do you think she's out with?" Skye asks.

"Someone who'll disappoint her," her father says. "Most likely."

"Last month there was a guy from her gym. But he was an idiot."

"Maybe she'll get lucky. Or lower her standards."

"I guess you can't stay here if she meets someone and, you know, wants to have him move in."

"What if I meet someone? Think she'd want to stay here?"

It turns out the cable doesn't reach all the way into the garage, so instead they have to prop the TV in the doorway and turn the love seat to face it. Verlaine doesn't look up when they lift it, only swivels an ear. Her father grimaces more often by the time they finish, and she picks up the cat so he can flop down. She pulls the coffee table close so he can prop his feet. Verlaine settles between them, tail against Skye's leg, head against her father's. They watch a comedy they've seen before, and half an hour in she forgets for a moment that they're in her mother's garage, forgets that the windows don't look out on huge old trees and a river of clear water bubbling down from the mountains over ancient rocks. Or she can pretend she's forgotten, which is good enough for now.

"You'll still be here next weekend, right?" she asks around

the awful itch that suddenly fills her throat, the saltiness of swallowed tears. She hasn't felt such tightness in her chest in almost a week, but now she isn't sure she can breathe at all.

The movie is still playing, but he glances away from the screen, gives her a look that isn't a smile or a frown but something strange and fragile—a mirror, she thinks, of her own. "Let's worry about next week," he says in the creaky voice that sounds as if it might not be here in a few hours, much less a few days, "when next week comes around."

He reaches over to squeeze her hand, but his knuckles brush Verlaine's head, and the cat stirs, stretches out a paw, digs claws into his thigh. He yanks his hand back.

An hour later, while they're watching the credits, she hears the front door of the house open and close, and then her mother's footsteps in the hall. She's alone, and her stride is slow—satisfied or vexed, Skye can't tell. But when she gets to the living room, she picks up her pace, and even before she reaches them, Skye and her father glance at each other, trying to hold their laughter back and then quickly sputtering.

"Who the hell stole my TV?" her mother calls.

ACKNOWLEDGMENTS

I AM ENORMOUSLY GRATEFUL to Laura Stanfill and Forest Avenue Press for believing in this book and bringing it into the world; to my students and colleagues at Willamette University and the Rainier Writing Workshop, who have taught me so much; to the stewards of Oregon's wild places, who tend the trails where I tramp and forage for fungus; to my family for putting up with all the hours I spend wandering the woods of my imagination; and to the editors of the publications where brief excerpts of the novel first appeared, in slightly different form:

Grist: A Journal of the Literary Arts
Willamette Magazine
One of Us: Stories (BKMK Press, 2020).

ABOUT THE AUTHOR

SCOTT NADELSON IS THE author of a novel, a memoir, and six collections of short fiction, most recently *While It Lasts*, recipient of the Donald L. Jordan Prize for Literary Excellence. His work has won an Oregon Book Award, the Great Lakes Colleges Association New Writers Award, and the Reform Judaism Fiction Prize and has been published in venues such as *Ploughshares, New England Review, Oregon Humanities, The Writer's Chronicle*, and *The Best American Short Stories*. He teaches at Willamette University, where he holds the Hallie Brown Ford Chair in Writing, and in the Rainier Writing Workshop MFA Program at Pacific Lutheran University.

READERS' GUIDE

1. Do the chapters in *Trust Me* function as individual stories in addition to forming a complete novel? What are some elements of a short story? Which chapters might make especially strong stories on their own? Why do you think so?

2. The novel alternates perspectives between father and daughter. Do you relate more to one character than the other? Why or why not?

3. *Trust Me* is a book about climate change; repercussions of years of environmental damage cause catastrophic consequences to the characters. Did you anticipate the fire sweeping through the novel? Have you lived through fire seasons? Or a dangerous meteorological event? How does it feel to be at the mercy of an uncontrollable force? Should Lewis have been more prepared? Are you prepared?

4. What is your impression of Veronica? Is your answer shaped more by her daughter's point of view, her ex-husband's perspective, or some of both?

5. Do you have a favorite tree? What makes it special?

6. Name some other novels you've read about divorce. Is there a strong sense of righteousness or side-taking, either from the characters' perspectives or through the narrator's lens? Compare those books with *Trust Me*. How do Lewis and Veronica handle talking about each other to their daughter? Does Lewis take responsibility for his flaws?

7. Discuss the title *Trust Me*. How does it reflect or engage with the themes of the novel?

8. Technology—the absence of a reliable cell signal—is part of why Lewis loves bringing Sills to the cabin. How does this lack of connectedness impact the quality of their time together? What are some of their favorite activities? Do you have tech-free routines built into your life? If not, have you thought about creating some?